THE EVENT AT FOURTEENTH AND U: A CHRISTMAS STORY

Calvin Davis

TRAFFORD PUBLISHING COMPANY
USA~Canada~United Kingdom~Ireland

This book is a work of fiction. Names, characters, places and incidents are either products of the author's imagination or are used fictiously. Any resemblance to actual events or locales or persons, living or dead, is entirely coincidental.

Printed in Victoria, Canada

Note for Librarians: a cataloguing record for this book that includes Dewey Classification and US Library of Congress numbers is available from the National Library of Canada. The complete cataloguing record can be obtained from the National Library's online database at: www.nlc-bnc.ca/amicus/index-e.html

ISBN 1-4120-1384-4

TRAFFORD

This book was published *on-demand* in cooperation with Trafford Publishing. On-demand publishing is a unique process and service of making a book available for retail sale to the public taking advantage of on-demand manufacturing and Internet marketing. **On-demand publishing** includes promotions, retail sales, manufacturing, order fulfilment, accounting and collecting royalties on behalf of the author.

Suite 6E, 2333 Government St., Victoria, B.C. V8T 4P4, CANADA

Phone	250-383-6864	Toll-free	1-888-232-4444 (Canada & US)
Fax	250-383-6804	E-mail	sales@trafford.com
Web site	www.trafford.com	TRAFFORD PUBLISHING IS A DIVISION OF TRAFFORD HOLDINGS LTD.	
Trafford Catalogue #03-1762		www.trafford.com/robots/03-1762.html	

10   9   8   7   6   5   4   3   2

To Vonnie and Mother

"He who has not Christmas in his heart will never find it under a tree."

-- Roy L. Smith

✳ *Chapter One*

Blustering Washington, DC winds sandblasted Willie Peterson as he closed the door of the welfare office. On the sidewalk he paused, sighed, pressed the collar of his tattered jacket to his neck, then, leaning into a whistling winter gust, headed home. Gradually his face contorted into a frown, for he knew that once home he would have to tell his pregnant wife, Louella, the bad news: the Migrant Assistance Fund, MAF, was out of money and thus was unable to provide help, not a dime. However, thanks to a gift from a local millionaire philanthropist, there would be a measure of relief, though pathetically small.

Like scores of other "emergency-needs" applicants, Willie was given seventy-five dollars in cash. The money was a one-time-only grant and the sole buffer between him and starvation or eviction -- or both.

When he reached Florida Avenue he turned left, passing tens of bars, diners, storefront churches and pool halls. He paused in front of Mattie Harris' Meal-land Restaurant. A makeshift wreath decorated its window, put together with aluminum foil, chicken wire and crepe paper. The lone customer at the counter slurped spareribs, sliding each across his lips as if playing a harmonica. Willie watched, struggling to muffle growls of hunger emanating from his stomach. Impossible, he thought. Sighing, he stuffed his cold hands into his pockets, leaned into stinging gusts and continued down Florida Avenue.

Minutes later, he entered the vacant lot at Florida and Fifth Street where several shabbily dressed men circled an open fire. Others stood a few yards away facing "Blind Reverend" Mary Sweetwater, a street preacher.

Soon after her graduation from divinity school, Mary lost her sight -- a victim of a rare eye disease. Her loss, she often said, was a blessing, heaven's way of directing her "to minister to the down-and-out, the earth's forgotten."

Daily the evangelist held services on the lot, her "church." After Willie walked to the fire to soak in some warmth, he turned to listen. "Today," the minister loudly proclaimed, "Christmas love and goodwill die *shameful* deaths. Both are now mere ceremony: exchanging cards, shopping, decorating trees and windows, all done with the coldness of a Wall Street broker."

"Ain't that the truth," the nondescript man in front of Willie blurted, "ain't that the gospel truth!"

"Yuletide presents, not love, are exchanged,"

Mary continued. "Today, Christmas music is the cold ring of cash registers, not the warm harmonies of love. And Christmas charity, where is it now, I ask you? Gone! Ancient history."

"Tell it like it is!" shouted a man brandishing a half empty wine bottle. "Tell it like--"

"But," the preacher said, voice solemn, "as surely as your eyes see and mine don't, the goodness of Christmas will *be restored.*"

"Amen!"

"I say again, restored. And *soon.*"

"Preach, Rev'! Preach!"

"In a vision, God in heaven revealed to me, a sightless common messenger, that The Redeemer Of Christmas will be here, here among us, come to restore Yuletide's goodness, mankind's hope."

"Here?" a doubter puzzled. "Among us?"

"How he gonna come, Reverend?" someone wondered.

"As a miracle baby, mothered by the most ordinary of women," the evangelist replied. "Born in poverty, among AIDS sufferers, boarded tenements and broken dreams."

"Rev', sound like you sure-'nough talking 'bout a neighborhood like this one, alright," someone shouted.

"Indeed," the preacher said. "Indeed."

"If this miracle baby show up in *this* neighborhood," one worshiper smirked, "he sure gonna need some miracles alright and lots of'em, too." Several in the congregation chuckled.

"Like John The Baptist," Mary stated,

"heaven's messengers are often ridiculed, their prophesies discounted. I expect no less. But mark my word, all I tell you shall come to pass.

"The Miracle Child will be born and, as I've stated, *restore* true Christmas to honor the birth of the Christ Child as it was meant to do. To the Doubting Thomases, I can only add--" Suddenly, the evangelist froze; her sightless eyes then probed emptiness.

"What's wrong, Rev'? Holy Ghost got your tongue?" More chuckles.

"Mock if you will," Mary said, "but I speak truth." Again she paused, her wrinkled hands now trembling. "Wait, wait, the father of the Miracle Child, I sense his presence. He is here, now, among us." The old woman, swooning, slumped to her knees and prayed. *"Heaven, if only for a moment, return vision, allow me to see the father of The Wonder Baby."*

"What's got into that woman?" someone mumbled.

"Beats me. Anyway, we still got a little wine left. Come on, let's down it."

"Good idea!"

After draining the bottle, the men, arm in arm, began bellowing "The Battle Hymn Of The Republic" -- out of tune -- then staggered towards Georgia Avenue, leaving the street preacher on her knees and Willie just in front of her.

"Ours will be," Mary sighed, "the happiest of times, when Christmas, true Christmas, joins goodness once more."

Willie approached the evangelist.
"Betta lemme help you up, lady. Otherwise, you gonna catch your death of cold on that ground, and that's for sure."

Mary slumped lower. Sobbing, she clutched Willie's pants legs and while smothering his battered shoes with kisses, she held on as if clinging to the final seconds of life. "Now I know peace," she moaned, eyes welling with tears, "for I have touched ...*greatness*."

Willie wrenched his legs free, then steadied the old woman to her feet. "You'll be alright, Rev'," he soothed, "be just fine."

When he was satisfied she would be, and after wiping tears from her cheeks, he headed down the sidewalk. At the corner he stopped and turned. Mary stared at him. Studying the street evangelist, Willie recalled her words: "I have touched greatness!"

Greatness? he puzzled. Him? Poor Willie Peterson? What did he have to do with greatness? Forcing back a laugh, he quickly reviewed his "inventory of greatness." Item one, he had no insurance for his pregnant wife's medical care. Two, he was jobless. Three, for income, such as it was, he scavenged aluminum cans, soda bottles and old newspapers from dumpsters and alleys and sold them for a few pennies per pound. In addition, he and his wife, weeks behind in rent payments, might be evicted any day. As for cash, he had but seventy-five dollars. How long would that last? Days? Hours? Minutes? Only God could tell. And if all these "items of greatness" weren't enough, his grocery supply was almost nonexistent -- a few loaves of molded, five-day-old bread, a slab of "fatback," and several damaged cans of generic vegetable soup.

Willie shook his head, dumbfounded. "What was with that old woman," he mumbled, "her with all that weird talk 'bout revelations, and some miracle kid fixing Christmas. Don't make no sense."

✳ *Chapter Two*

Robert Lucas Johnson would have been the last person on earth to believe the prophesy of a street preacher. He didn't believe in divine messages or, for that matter, in a divinity -- of any kind. Nor did he subscribe to universal brotherhood or the spirit of charity accompanying the Christmas season. Robert, who preferred to be called by his professional name, Snake, didn't believe in much of anything -- except money. Not being particular from where it came, or whose it was, as long as it ended up in *his* pocket.

Snake was a combination con man and street hustler, talented in a variety of slick scams: the flim-flam, winning lottery ticket gyp, cheap TV bunco, the ole hot watch trick, etc.

Fellow hustlers said he was at his virtuoso best when working the cheap TV bunco. In this, Snake approached an unsuspecting patsy and, hinting the item was "hot," enticed him into buying a "spank brand new RCA 31 incher." The flim flammer said he had the merchandise in the trunk of his car --

"still in the carton, too." He offered the TV at a "giveaway" price of only fifty dollars. Why so cheap? His "wife," he claimed, needed an operation -- cancer. Or sometimes his "son" was dying of the same disease or a liver infection -- whichever worked. When the customer opened the container, he discovered he'd just bought a cardboard box and a large rock at the "bargain" price of fifty dollars. By then Snake was in his car and gone -- having to "rush to the hospital," he explained.

The rip-off he worked on Widow Flossie Robinson Snake considered his "master stroke." The eighty-six year old woman lived alone in a rundown rooming house on Thirteenth Street. One morning Snake, outfitted in a clergyman's collar (stolen), knocked on her door. After flashing "proper identification" (forged), he claimed he was a missionary for a church in Baltimore and urged her to make a contribution to "The Save The Starving Children Of Ethiopia Foundation." The visitor informed that he was the group's founder and president. Gloating, he spoke of the hundreds of zombie-like children nourished back to health because of his organization's "marvelous fund raising campaigns."

Within an hour, the "charity founder" conned the old woman into withdrawing every dime from her savings account -- two thousand, sixty two dollars and twenty cents. With her "generous contribution," Snake doubled payments on his Cadillac that month.

Soon thereafter, the widow, penniless, was evicted. On Christmas Eve, with temperatures hovering near freezing, her belongings were piled on the sidewalk. The following morning, a policeman, Officer Carlos Sanchez, found Mrs. Robinson lying on her sofa. Thieves had stolen everything else -- chairs, tables, lamps, even her wedding band. The cop thought she was just another drunk sleeping one off, or some addict stoned senseless. The old woman, of course, was neither. With her eyes clamped shut, the octogenarian had frozen to death.

While playing eight ball for twenty dollars a game at Fat Tucker's Pool Emporium two days later, Snake learned of the widow's death as two players at the next table bemoaned her "sad passing." As they chatted, Snake yawned. He then leaned over the pool table and, taking careful aim, kissed the eight ball off the six. The eight inched towards the side pocket -- "kaplunk."

"Rack'em, Four-eyes," Snake grinned as he spoke to the house man, "look like I just bagged another chump."

"Don't you always, Snake?"

"Four-eyes, lemme tell-ya some'm': world's a jungle. The strong take from the weak, smart from the strong. Life's tough but fair." Snake placed his cue stick in the rack. "Catch-cha later, Four-eyes," he said, swaggering towards the door.

"Sure thing, tiger."

Outside, Snake grinned. He was elated that fate had anointed him one of the "smart" of the world, able to take his "share" -- more if possible -- from both the strong and the weak, though he preferred "working" the weak, people like Widow Robinson... the easy marks.

Willie met Snake at the intersection of Florida Avenue and Sixth Street where, now chilled, Willie joined several men circled around a steel drum filled with flaming two-by-fours. Snake was among them.

"Merry Christmas," Willie greeted.

"Same to-ya," a man to his right smiled.

"Yeah, merry Christmas," another mumbled.

Snake said nothing. He was too busy eyeballing Willie, hoping to determine if the stranger could possibly be his next patsy.

"Broke as I am," one of the men said, "I sure don't know how merry my Christmas gon' be. I'm broke, busted, got 'bout ten cents to my name."

"Well," Willie smiled, "look at it this way: ya still got ya health and strength, and that's the greatest of Christmas presents."

"Well, ya might have a point."

The men glanced at Snake, who continued to "read" Willie. Aware of the con man's intentions and wanting no part of the scheme, they left.

"And what did you say your name is?" Snake grinned.

"Didn't, but it's Willie Peterson."

"Where-ya from, Willie?"

"Big Island, Virginia. Ever hear of it?"

"Nope."

"That ain't surprising."

"Why-ya say that?"

"Big Island's just a little truck stop, as different from a city like Washington, DC as day is from night."

"That's good," Snake said, delighted that the small town bumpkin would be an easy mark. "Real good."

"Pardon. Ah, what did you say?"

"Ah, I said 'that's good, real good.' That is, it's good to make your acquaintance."

"Oh. Same here. Tell me, what's your name?"

"Robert Johnson, but most call me by my nickname."

"What's that?"

"Snake. Now wait, before you think the wrong thing, maybe I'd betta explain. You see, my daddy was a religious man, like myself. He was a preacher in the hills of West Virginia, a snake handler. During his services, he handled quite a few snakes, one too many as it turned out -- God rest his soul. Anyway," Snake lied, "that's how I got my name: ya see, first they called me, 'Snake Junior,' then just plain 'Snake.'"

"I see. You know, fooling 'round with rattlers and copperheads is a real dangerous thing."

"Not if you have faith in the holy word."

"I take it you do."

"All the way. Not only does I believe The Good Book, but I *live* by it, too. But enough 'bout me. What 'bout yourself? Tell me, how's Santa gonna treat you this Christmas?" Snake asked, hoping to discover if Willie had any money.

As Willie told of his financial woes, the "son of the snake handler" palmed back a yawn. But when he mentioned the seventy-five dollars he carried, Snake's eyes lit. "Guess I'll use the money to make part payment on my rent, buy 'nough food to tide me and my wife over for a day-a two," Willie said, "and then get her a little Christmas gift -- can't spend much on it though -- just a token to let her know that broke or not, I still got Christmas love in my heart for her."

"Now ain't that nice. Yeah, the ole Christmas love, ya sure don't want to never lose that," Snake counseled. "It's something folks could always use more of, always."

"Peace on earth and good will to men," Willie inserted.

"That *sure* cover it all, don't it? Sad, but today, people are getting away from Christmas values. You know, brotherhood, love thy neighbor as thyself, stuff like that," Snake lamented, placing his hand on Willie's shoulder and smiling, as if the two were brothers.

Ten minutes later, Snake, having picked Willie's pocket, strode down Florida Avenue counting and recounting the victim's seventy-five dollars. Once convinced he hadn't been "shortchanged," Snake slipped the bills into his wallet and continued towards North Capital Street. Where it intersected Florida Avenue stood a Salvation Army worker manning a kettle.

"Help the needy. Remember the poor."

"Merry Christmas!" Snake smiled, eying the kettle, which brimmed with money.

"Same to-ya, sir. Season's blessings." Startled by a van screeching to a halt at a stoplight, the charity agent pivoted to see what was happening. Seconds later, he turned to continue chatting with the friendly stranger. He couldn't. The friendly stranger was gone -- so was the kettle of money.

Immediately the solicitor hailed a passing policeman, who gave chase. No contest. Even weighted by a cast iron kettle of coins, Snake left the lawman in the dust.

The victimized Salvation Army worker was fortunate: he discovered his loss immediately. Willie wasn't so lucky. Not until he was several blocks from home did he realize his seventy-five dollars was gone. So skillfully had Snake picked his pocket, the victim had no idea what happened to the money.

Blocks away, Willie's wife lay across the bed, hands cupped over her eyes. She felt queasy. The contents of her stomach she envisioned spewing from her like water from a faucet. She stared anxiously at her abdomen. Its bulge was pronounced, reminding her she was nine months pregnant. As if she needed a reminder. For hers had been a very painful pregnancy: morning sickness, hemorrhoids, fierce pain and, without cash or health insurance, not a single visit to a doctor.

"Bam! Bam! Bam!" Someone pounded the door.

"Yeah."

"It's me, Mr. Ferguson, the landlord."
"Oh."
"I'm sure you know why I'm here."
"I think I do."
"Look, I don't have to tell-ya, you people are three *whole* weeks behind in rent."
"You right, Mr. Ferguson, you don't have to tell me that."
"I gotta have the money and soon."
"I know that, and I wants to get it to you, too, and I plan to, quick as I can. Lately, Mr. Ferguson, times've been hard for my husband and me, real hard, even worse now that's it's almost Christmas, and we ain't gone have a good one, that's for sure. Anyway, he busted his back, can't do no heavy work; all he can do is collect junk. As for me, I'm pregnant. Baby might be born any day."
"None-a what-cha say is news, Mrs. Peterson."
"I thought maybe you'd forgotten."
"No, I ain't forgot: I do understand your situation."
"I see." A leaden silence followed. "Anyway, I was wondering, Mr. Ferguson, wondering if you could find it in your heart to bear with Willie and me just a *little* while longer, 'til we back on our feet again?"
"I'm sorry 'bout the accident your husband had on his job, Mrs. Peterson, really am. It's a real *sad* thing. But that don't change the fact you still owe me money."
"You're right, don't change that fact at all. Anyway, Willie, he's at the welfare office now, went

to find out if they can give us some kinda special 'sistance. Also, if they're handing out them free Christmas food baskets this year."

"About them baskets, Mrs. Peterson, I can answer that for you right now. No."

"You mean, they ain't?"

"Article about it was in the paper yesterday. Money ran out."

"Now ain't that a crying shame! And we was counting on them baskets. Well, my Willie, he should be home pretty soon now."

"I hope he's gonna bring some good news."

"You ain't the only one."

"'Cause if he don't, I'm afraid I'll be forced to do something that ain't pleasant."

"I--"

"I expect you know what I'm talking about."

"Yes, sir, 'fraid I do."

"If I'm forced to, I'll set your stuff on the sidewalk. To be honest, doing that won't bring me no pleasure, 'cause both you and your husband seem like decent folks. But what can I do, Mrs. Peterson? I mean, business is business, you understand that. Anyway, if I set your stuff out, I can tell-ya now it ain't gonna be pretty. You've probably seen what happens."

"Too many times, Mr. Ferguson."

"People turn into savages, battling over everything they can lay hands on. So I hope I won't have to--."

"Me too, Mr. Ferguson."

"Same to-ya."

"What was that, Mr. Ferguson?"

"Sorry, Mrs. Peterson. I said, 'Same to-ya,' but I wasn't talking to you. A tenant was passing in the hall, and she wished me a merry Christmas, and I said, 'Same to you.'"

"Oh. So you was wishing somebody else a merry Christmas, uh?"

"Yes, m'am. Anyway, like I was telling-ya, I hope you and your husband can come up with the money. I'd hate to have to lose you as tenants."

"Kind of you to say that," she groaned as she ungracefully sat on one of the two kitchen chairs,

"My pleasure. And ah, by the way, Mrs. Peterson."

"Yes, sir."

"If I don't talk to-ya no more before the The Day Of Love, I hope you have a merry Christmas." He waited for Louella's response. "Did you hear what I said, Mrs. Peterson? Ah, I said I hope-ya have a--"

"I heard."

"Oh." The landlord cleared his throat. "For a second I thought maybe you hadn't... Anyway, have a good day."

"Good day? Well, under these circumstances, Mr. Ferguson, I'll do the best I can."

"I'm sure you will."

As Mr. Ferguson trudged down the stairs, Louella looked across the room past the dilapidated bed, the thrift-store-bought chest of drawers and the wobbly chair near the window, two of its legs propped up with old books. Straining to overcome the weight of the new life she carried, she arose, steadied herself, then plodded to the window and looked down.

A crowd clogged the sidewalk. Some were unemployed day laborers, others panhandlers and homeless men in search of shelter. A few derelicts loitered near the entrance of Theodore's Bar And Grill. Occasionally the door of the popular watering hole opened. Through it gushed a mixture of chatter, laughter and sobbing saxophones, as inside, Bill Harris' Capital Expressways played "White Christmas," mournfully, as if the melody were a Delta blues tune.

On the window ledge of Big Bargain Used Furniture Store sat an old street singer, Sister Rosetta. Her wrinkled fingers chorded an aged guitar. "S-i-i-i-i-lent night..." she moaned.

Louella inched back to the bed and lay across it. The queasiness she felt earlier returned. Tormented by it, she lay still, listening as the voice of the street singer meandered into the room.

"...Ho-o-o-ly...night..."

A serrated arrow of agony darted through her womb.

"...Al-l-l-l is cal-l-l-m-m-m-m. A-l-l is bright..."

The pain assaulting Louella was double-edged, biting.

"...'Round yon vir-r-r-r-gin, mother and..."

The pain Louella felt streaked through her like jolts of electricity.

"Sle-e-e-p in..."

Wincing, Louella's closed her eyes.

"Hea-a-a-a-venly pe-e-e-e-a-ce...sl-e-e-e-p in heavenly peace."

Soon after Willie left the lot where Blind Mary preached, the temperature plummeted and wind lashed like whips. Two blocks later, he stopped beside a lot covered with mounds of Christmas trees. "Can make-ya a fine price on one-a them trees," the vendor smiled. "Guaranteed to bring the season's spirit to you and the misses."

"I--"

"All genuine firs, too, fresh cut, got my word on that."

"What's your asking price?" Willie said, more to make conversation than a serious inquiry.

"Small ones, five dollars. Big ones, eight."

"Ah, think not."

"I can even make you a better deal on one-a them smaller trees -- say, three fifty. How that sound?"

"Fair 'nough, but even that's too rich for my blood." Willie turned.

"Wait, mista! Ain't you gonna at least take a closer look at one or two of my trees?" Willie stopped. "Look, tell-ya what I'll do, I'll cut the price on a couple of big ones and --"

"Mista."

"Yeah."

"If you was selling them trees for a quarter a piece, I couldn't afford a twig."

"You *are* joking, ain't-cha?"

"Do I look like I am?" Willie said, voice as

somber as his face.

"I understand."

"Mista, I wish you did, I really do. I mean, here it is Christmas time, time for giving, sharing, and I can't afford a tree for my family, not even the smallest on your lot -- let alone a Christmas present for my wife. And you tell me you understand?"

"Well, ah what I mean is..."

Before the vendor could finish the sentence, Willie turned and headed home.

✱ *Chapter Three*

Soon Willie stood in front of 4545 Fourteenth Street, the tenement where he lived. Groping for answers, his thoughts waded through murky pools. The mystery, of course, was what had happened to the seventy-five dollars. He remembered putting it into his pocket. He knew he had, *knew* it. But now, every dime, as if by magic, was gone. Gone? But where to? And how had it disappeared?

Willie closed his eyes, hoping to calm the cyclone raging inside. He needed to sort through the maze of jumbled facts, to somehow come up with a plausible explanation. There had to be one, just had to. Maybe the envelope containing the money had fallen out of his pocket. Or perhaps he lost it when he knelt or accidentally brushed against someone. Or, who knows, a passing gust might have plucked it free.

When he walked into his room, Louella was lying on the bed, silent, studying the gaping hole in

the ceiling.
"How-ya doing, hon'?"
"I'm OK, Lou'." After breezing a kiss off her cheek, he paused near the foot of the bed and fidgeted. Soon, he marshaled his courage, then blurted what he believed was the truth about the missing seventy-five dollars -- that he had somehow lost it. "Baby, I'm sorry...really I'm--"
"Willie."
"Yeah?"
"You don't have to apologize."
"It's just that I feel so guilty."
"Hush," she soothed, "...just hush."
"But, Lou'--"
"Willie, now listen: there be no more guilty talk, you hear?"
"I feel awful, worthless."
"I know you didn't *mean* to lose that money. It was, it was a accident, Willie. Folks have'm every day."
"True, but that aside, I'd sure like to know when hard times and bad luck gonna leave us 'lone? When? God knows we've had our share. Plus, to make things worser, this latest misfortune is coming at, of *all* times, Christmas, when you and me, Lou', we ought-ta be celebrating."
"Willie, I understand how you feel. But, believe me, in the end everything'll turn out alright. We'll both be just fine, you'll see."
"Lou', you really think that?"
"Sure I do, as sure as we're conversating. Listen, you and me, Willie, we've made it through

many-a hard time before. You know that. Many."

"More than I can count," he sighed in resignation.

"And somehow, we overcame'm. So, don't go fretting and putting yourself down over that money. Don't."

He paused. "Lou'?"

"Yeah, Willie."

"You know somethin'?"

"What?"

"When God made you, he sure put together one hell of a woman."

Relieved that the "truth" about the "lost" money was finally out, Willie began telling Louella of his trip to the welfare office. He spoke of the endless lines there, the arrogance of the clerks, their snapping impatience. Finally, he mentioned Blind Reverend Mary and her strange prophesy. Listening attentively, Louella, stared at the far wall. "Why so quiet, Lou'? I say something wrong?"

"No, won't that." Facing him, she sighed, "Willie."

"Huh?"

"You sure the preacher lady said them things 'bout me and my baby?"

"'Course."

"Well, there's something I never told you 'fore, Willie. Fact, never told a soul. But after what you just said, maybe I should."

"Oh?"

"Then again, I ain't sure I ought-ta share this with nobody."

"Me included, Lou'?"

"You included, Willie."

"Why?"

"Oh, I don't know," she shrugged, "I mean, it's just that--"

"Look, Lou', we've always been open with each other. Ain't we?"

"Always."

"I can't see no reason for changing that now."

"In my heart I know you're right. Really, I do."

"Besides, you'll probably feel better if you let it out."

"Well, I suppose telling you can't really do no harm." Louella focused on the scarred floor, staring as if vision could penetrate wood. Finally she sighed, "Willie."

"Yeah."

"You remember where my family lived in Big Island, don't-cha? In them backwoods, near Loc's Mountain."

"'Course I do."

"Well, that's where it happened. At the time I was only 'bout three or four, too young to understand. My momma, she later told me all 'bout it. Said one day this group of Gypsies stopped at our shack -- a old woman and her two sons. Momma asked'em why they was so far from the main highway, that nobody hardly, 'cept coon hunters, ever came back in them hollows. The mother of the group -- a wrinkled woman named Della -- she explained that for over a year she'd heard strange voices calling her in the night, hounding her, directing her and her sons to our shack.

"'But why here, why us?' Momma wanted to know. 'We just poor country folks squeezing out a living on rocky land that can't hardly grow nothing.'

"'Why?' the old Gypsy woman said. 'It's because of your daughter.'

"'My daughter?'

"'Yes, her.'

"'Is there something wrong with Louella? Has somebody put a spell on her? What bad things is gonna befall my child? Tell me! Don't spare me the truth. I hear you folks can read the future. So go on, tell me. Is Louella gonna be sick, suffer from cancer maybe?'

"Momma said the Gypsy woman stared at her for a while, then said, 'No, your child's not the one that'll be sick, but others at Christmas will be, those diseased with coldness and greed. And your daughter will give birth to the cure.'"

Willie scratched his head. "Lou."

"Yeah."

"That sure was curious talk by Della, won't it?"

"Curiser than I've ever heard."

"Wonder what it all mean?"

Louella looked at her husband, eyes full of wonder. "Willie, for years now I asked myself that very same question. Just what does it all mean? And, Willie, I ain't found no answer yet."

Christmas gift."

"Christmas gift, Shorty?"

"Yeah, I mean, the way you helped me sober up. Without you, Mary, I'd probably be laying in some gutter right now, stoned, instead of sober and looking forward to Christmas...with hope."

"The credit belongs to you, Shorty, not me."

"Mary, your modesty is as big as your heart."

Shorty helped his friend board the bus, then guided her to a seat near the entrance. "Driver, mind letting Reverend Mary off at the home of Bishop Richfield?"

"Home?" the bus driver chuckled. "You mean, castle, don't-cha?"

"You're right there. A castle *is* more like it. Anyway, do ya' mind?"

"Happy to."

Twenty minutes later the driver announced, "This here's your stop, Rev'. Ah, you need help?"

"No, thanks, I believe I can manage."

"Sure?"

"Quite."

Mary felt her way to the exit. Seeing a passing postman, the driver hailed him and asked if he'd escort the evangelist to Bishop Richfield's residence. He agreed.

Standing before the portal of the palatial home, Mary raised the ornate brass knocker with her gloved hand. "Bam...Bam...Bam!" Soon, the door opened and a middle-aged woman, face chiseled from granite, appeared. Her maid's uniform was spotless, impeccably pressed.

✳ *Chapter Four*

The following morning Blind Reverend Mary, white cane in hand, groped east along Seventh Street."

"Tap...tap...tap..."

Using her cane, she tattooed the curb, making sure she hadn't strayed too close to the street. A misstep could result in injury, a fact she knew well, for the previous year she had tripped and toppled into the path of a swerving Yellow Cab. The result was a fractured ankle and a month's convalescence in DC General Hospital.

"Tap...tap...tap..."

Mary hated hospitals, in fact, she hated all things confining. In spite of her blindness, she enjoyed being unfettered, active: she relished rising early, walking to her "church," preaching, conversing with friends, visiting the sick, going here and there. She was an independent, liberated spirit. She never had to remind herself of this -- others, yes, and often, especially those who saw her as helpless.

"Tap...tap...tap..."

Now at the bus stop. she heard footsteps to her rear.

"Morn', Rev'."

"Morning, 'Shorty.'"

Shorty's legal name was Stratton Louis Allepo. Along Florida Avenue, however, everyone knew him as "Shorty." The middle-aged mail clerk was once a lush. For months, off and on, Mary counseled him, hoping to help her friend conquer his drinking problem. During his many relapses, three or more a month, she braced him with patience and understanding, encouraging him to have faith in his potential. Finally, he did. And thanks to Mary, he hadn't touched the bottle in over a year.

"How-ya like this weather, Shorty?"

"Too windy for me."

"Same here."

"I'm all for a white Christmas, yes, but freezing winds I can do without."

"Shorty, like you, most people adore white Christmases; they retrieve memories of old friends and good times."

"No doubt 'bout that. By the way, Mary, kinda odd seeing you this far down on Seventh Street."

"Had to come here to transfer to the Number Seven bus."

"Where-ya headed?"

"Upper New Hampshire Avenue. I've got some important business there, Shorty. It's urgent I talk to Bishop Richfield."

"Bishop Richfield?"

"Yes."

"You don't mean *The* Bishop Donald Richfield, do you, pastor of that church in the ritzy section of New Hampshire Avenue?"

"The same."

"Well, never figured you and The Bishop would have all that much in common, Mary. I mean, he's, you know, upper crust and all."

"So I'm told."

"Think you'll feel comfortable in that, ah, *silk stocking* neighborhood?"

"I'm sure I will, thanks to the blessing God gave me."

"Blessing?"

"Yes. Blindness, Shorty. Blindness. You see, to the blind, all neighborhoods are the same. Anyway, as I said, today I have crucial news I must share with The Bishop."

"You make it sound like it's a matter of life and death, Mary."

"It is, Shorty -- the most *important* news ever heard."

"You mean, heard by The Bishop, don't-cha?"

"No, Shorty...heard by *the world.*"

"Well now, if I ain't being too nosey, Mary, what is this important news?"

"Be happy to tell you. You see--"

"Scre-e-e-e-ch..." At the icy curb a Metro Transit Authority bus jerked to a stop.

"It's your bus, Mary -- Number Seven."

"At last."

"Before you go, wanna thank you for my

"Yes?" she iced.

"I was wondering if--"

"Are you at the right address?" the woman asked, eying Mary's unimpressive attire with obvious disdain.

"This is where Bishop Richfield lives, isn't it?"

"Yes, it is, but, ah, I expect it may not be the address *you're* looking for."

"If The Bishop lives here, this is it."

"It is, huh?"

"Like to speak to him, please."

"Do you have an appointment?"

"No."

"Nothing personal, you understand, but the Bishop rarely grants audiences at this hour, and to those without appointments, never."

"Just tell him Reverend Sweetwater is here. I think he'll make an exception."

"You certain of that?"

"Yes, quite."

"Well, I don't know."

Sighing, the blind woman said, "Please, would you be so kind as to tell him I'm here?"

"I can tell you now you're wasting your time, but if you insist. Wait."

"Inside?"

"No."

The door snapped shut just as a punishing frigid gust whipped past. Mary pressed the collar of her threadbare coat to her neck and bristled.

Soon, the door reopened. Before her towered Bishop Reverend Donald Richfield. Over six feet and weighing at least two hundred and fifty pounds, the religious leader was imposing. His suit, charcoal gray and tailored in the fashionable Italian style, cuddled his frame like a kid glove.

"Wel-l-l-l," he boomed, "if it isn't my old college classmate, Mary, Mary Sweetwater! My, it's good to see you, so *good*. Been ages. Ah, don't just stand there, Mary. Come in, it's freezing out there."

He ushered the unexpected guest inside. Holding her at arms length, he scanned the blind woman and smiled. "My, you're looking just wonderful, absolutely wonderful. And you don't appear to be a day older than when you were a coed."

"No older, you say? Donald, I thought in your profession you dealt in truth." Both laughed.

The mahogany-paneled study to which the noted religious leader escorted his guest was cavernous. Its oak flooring sparkled, almost as brightly as the crystal chandelier suspended above it. The Bishop eased Mary into the lushness of a Vanderbilt and Roth Comfort Chair, directly in front of which warmth radiated from a crackling fireplace.

"Certainly feels good in here, Donald."

"It's the fireplace, Mary. A few burning logs make all the difference in the world."

"That's for sure."

For almost an hour the friends reminisced about the undergraduate days they shared. Finally, the Bishop said, "So, tell me, what brings you to the home of an old country preacher like myself?"

Mary told of the revelation she had and how in

an instant it came. "Like a sunburst, Donald. And though I couldn't see it, I felt its presence. And then I heard a voice. 'My blind servant,' it said, 'The Christmas Child will soon arrive, born to regenerate Yuletide. Your mission is to tell all of its coming.'"

"Mary, yours is an exemplary life. I can think of no worthier one to announce the good tidings."

"Exemplary? No, Donald, I have done nothing special."

"After all these years, your modesty, Mary, is as great as ever. Tell me, could I assist you in any way?"

"Well, I'll need someone to help me spread the word. And you're in a good position to do that. I'm told you have about eight hundred members in your church."

"Closer to a thousand."

"All the better. I'd like you to share my message with your flock and have them pass it on. And while you're spreading the news in your church, I'll do the same in mine -- on street corners, bars, barber shops, alleys."

"So that's how I can help, uh?"

"If you'd be so kind."

The Bishop smiled. "Mary."

"Yes."

"Why, of course I'll help. I'm honored you asked"

"Bless you, Donald, bless you."

Mary said she hated to, but she'd have to leave, for she planned to spend the remainder of the day spreading her message.

"Look, if you'd like, I'd be more than happy to drop you off somewhere, Mary."

"Would you, Donald?"

"My pleasure."

He led her to his two-car garage. The maid who'd "welcomed" Mary stood near the door.

"Be back shortly, Cindy."

"I'll have your usual snack ready, sir," the servant beamed. Cindy's smile was for The Bishop. The glare that followed had Mary's name etched all over it.

"You're so kind, Cindy," The Bishop said. "So kind."

"Well, I try, sir," she glowed.

Cradling Mary's arm, Donald helped her to his limousine, the latest model Lincoln Luxury Limited; his other vehicle, his favorite, a Mercedes 300, was in the repair shop -- sticky valves. He nosed the silver Lincoln onto New Hampshire Avenue, wheeled left, then headed towards Downtown Washington.

"Where do you want me to drop you off?"

"Seventh and Liberty."

"In front of that big rooming house?"

"No, a few doors down, at Kim's Barber Shop. Know where it is?"

"I think I do."

"Good. I figured Kim's Shop is the best place to start. Barbershops are excellent for disseminating news, even better than *The Washington Post*."

"More colorful, too."

"Always," Mary chuckled.

Donald turned onto Columbia Road. Purring,

the sleek limousine cruised past row after row of rundown tenements, some modestly decorated for the season: homemade wreaths, strips of aluminum foil, tattered ribbons, all taped to doors. Through shadeless windows, skeleton-like Christmas trees could be seen, their tiny lights almost a mockery of the season. On the sidewalk near Liberty Avenue a row of garbage cans sat. Two elderly "bag ladies" rummaged through them. Finding nothing edible, they trudged on.

Finally, the Lincoln eased to a stop in front of Kim's Barber Shop. The Bishop walked to the passenger side and helped Mary out. "Thank you, Donald."

"You're certainly welcome, my friend." He paused, started to speak, then stopped and sighed. To the intuitive woman, the intermission seemed unnaturally long.

"Donald?" she gently inquired.

"Yes."

"Are you...are you alright?"

"Why, of course I am. Well, if you want to know the truth, Mary, no, I'm not alright."

"What's the matter?"

"Well, you see, I..." he stopped and sighed.

"Go on, Donald."

"Listen, something has been bothering me off and on for quite a while, even more now that Christmas is nearly here."

"What?"

"Mary, I sometimes drive past the lot where you preach. I see you there, like a mother hen

tending her brood of, so called, 'undesirables.' And
I admit that each time I pass, especially during this
season, I nearly choke with shame."

"Why?"

"Because, Mary, in my heart I know I should
be on that lot with you, or at some similar place
ministering to the downtrodden, as The Master
taught, not motoring past in a limousine en route to
a luxury parsonage."

"You really shouldn't feel that way."

"I wish I didn't. God knows I wish I didn't,
Mary, but--"

"Friend, don't torture yourself, and certainly
not during Yuletide, the time of joy and exultation.
Listen, in The Father's vineyard each, according to
his talents, is assigned a task.

"Yours is to guide your congregation, for,
though most are well off, they too, like the poor,
need a shepherd. And, Donald, you are that
shepherd. Would you deny your flock spiritual
guidance because they're affluent or live in a certain
neighborhood? Donald, we all have our heavenly
job descriptions. You, yours, I, mine. Mine is to
minister to the lowly. Yours to..." Mary "looked" at
her former classmate. Her voice gentled, "Don."

"Yes."

"Mind stepping over here to me, please?" The
noted church leader hesitated. When he finally inched
closer, Mary circled her arms around him. "It's OK,
Donald," she comforted, "it's OK. Just remember,
each is given a task. And God, I'm sure, wants you
to perform yours without shame or guilt."

The Bishop tensed, then gradually relaxed. "Mary."

"Yes?"

"Most would never guess it, but from time to time, even the pastor of a huge one thousand member congregation needs a little warmth and understanding."

"Don't we all, Donald?"

Inside Kim's Barbershop, "Crap" Holmes stood in the center of the floor. Unofficial entertainer-in-residence, he chronicled yet another of his Don Juan tall tales. "And this woman -- *fine* too, like a movie star -- kept begging me to date her."

"Yea, sure, Crap, we believe you," someone grinned.

In the back room several men played cards.

"Hell!" one boomed, "you can't use that Jack-a diamond, Slick! You damn shithead!"

Kim, the shop's owner, glanced up, and seeing Mary enter, hurriedly frowned Crap into silence, then said, "Skeeta, step back there and tell them boys stop all that damn, ah, I mean, tone down the rowdiness. We got company -- a lady of the cloth."

Skeeta quickly complied, and when the card players emerged from the back room, each sheepishly lowered his head. "Sorry, Rev', we didn't mean no harm," one mumbled.

"None done," Mary assured. "Gentlemen, let us pray." Everyone bowed his head, even Crap, notorious for defying authority, especially policemen, which accounted for the bandage now circling his head.

Having finished her prayer, she told of the pending Miracle Birth, indicating it would take place somewhere in the neighborhood.

"What?" Crap gasped, hands on his hips. "In *this* neighborhood?"

"Don't make no kinda sense!" somebody observed.

"Sure don't!"

"Fact, it's 'bout the dumbest damn..." -- the speaker suddenly remembered a preacher was present -- "ah, I mean, the oddest thing I ever heard."

"Heed my words," Mary assured, "for what I tell you is *exactly* as Providence revealed it to me."

"But, Rev'," Kim said, scratching his head, "you can't seriously mean in a neighborhood like this. I mean, look 'round you. What-cha see? Junked cars, boarded tenements, littered streets and folks who ain't got nothing, including hope."

"And why not in this neighborhood?" Mary said. "In fact, of *all* neighborhoods on earth, what more fitting one than this?"

Hours later, as twilight silhouetted the Washington Monument and ribbons of cars crept across Fourteenth Street Bridge en route to suburban Northern Virginia, Mary felt her way into her room.

Having spent most of the day heralding news of the Glorious Event, the aging preacher was exhausted. She had tapped a path over much of

Florida Avenue and lower Seventh Street. The preacher was unaccustomed to such long sojourns. However, she knew it was imperative that her assigned mission be completed, and soon -- regardless of the price her body would pay.

She sat on the edge of the bed and exhaled deeply, fearful that air streaming from her nostrils was siphoning the remaining remnants of her energy.

Across the street, a neon sign announced the location of The Capitol Tourist Home. The sign's illumination, streaking amber, merged with the faraway sound of chimes that whispered "Silent Night."

The melody reminded Mary of a Christmas morning years earlier and of a music box under her family's tree. She was a child at the time and had full vision. The image of that morning was indelible. She especially recalled the tree. It sat in the middle of the living room. Beneath it were stacks of presents. Beside them, a music box. The melody it played was "Silent Night."

Because of what happened next, Mary could never forget that morning when, eyes wide, she skipped down the hall stairs. Eager for the arrival of Santa, she hadn't slept well -- twisting, turning, nerves tingling anticipation. But finally, the moment had come -- time to open her gifts. She sat under the tree and began unwrapping them. Above her, tree lights twinkled, dotting the room with sparkle.

"Br-r-r-r-r...br-r-r-r-r-r!" The telephone that sat on the hall table rang. Mary's father answered it, and shortly thereafter approached his daughter with news she did not want to hear. "Child, your mother is dead; she was killed in an auto accident."

Elizabeth, Mary's mother, had gotten up early that morning to prepare Christmas dinner, a task which usually consumed most of the day. Though the work was exhausting, she delighted in doing it. Cooking Christmas dinner from scratch was her way of translating her love into edibles. Needing some vanilla flavoring for the Christmas cake, she walked down the street to a convenience store.

At the corner, a red Corvette darted through a stop light. Swerving, it slammed into the curb, bounding over it. Tires squealed, one exploding -- "Boom!" The driver's head rammed the windshield, reducing the glass partition to a heap of fragments on the demolished hood. The Corvette had pinned Mary's mother against a brick wall.

Soon, paramedics arrived. One knelt beside the dead woman. Then, wincing, he looked away.

"Mary," her father said, "Christmas, I know, is a time for giving, but for heaven to ask you, a child, to contribute *so* much, is beyond my human understanding." He gazed into his daughter's eyes. There he saw the unintended hurt his words had caused. "I guess what I really meant, child, was...on this Christmas Day, God borrowed your mother. Yes, borrowed her. He needed her sweetness in heaven, needed it there, beside Him. So, God requested her as a loan. I'm sure at some future time, on a Christmas Day like this perhaps, He'll repay the debt with generous interest, the kind only God can give."

The words consoled Mary. For years they remained vaulted in her memory. Only as Mary sat on the bed that night hearing Christmas chimes play in the distance was she able to retrieve them.

She creaked to her knees. Placing her elbows on the edge of the bed and bowing her head, she prayed.

"Father, having borrowed my mother, you, I know, make my burdens heavy to prepare me for the present assignment. During this Yuletide, I hope to fulfill that mission, and, sightless, guide those with eyes to see that true Christmas will be reborn. If this is my task, grant me strength, patience and endurance. For I will need them all." She paused. "These things I pray in the holy name of Jesus. Amen."

Later, she lay in her narrow bed. Gradually her face lit. "Perhaps," she whispered, "perhaps, future Christmases will at last be reunited with charity, love and hope."

"Or," she heard a mysterious voice intone, "perhaps not. And Christmas will remain what it is today; a ritual, once filled with devout meaning, but now reduced to nothing."

✳ *Chapter Five*

Two days later, "Skipper" McCormick rushed into the office of Mr. Jack Lee Kinkade, managing editor of the *Washington Post's* "City" section. Seated in front of a Macintosh computer, the veteran newsman fine-tuned his latest editorial.

"Mr. Kinkade!" The young Skipper exploded, "Mr. Kinkade, sir, I--"

"Slow down, Skipper. In the name of normal blood pressure -- yours *and* mine -- will-ya *kindly* slow *down.*"

"Sure, Mr. Kinkade, sir," Skipper panted, "...I'll...I'll try!"

Seconds later. "Well, now that you've gotten a hold of yourself, what's the problem, son?"

"Mr. Kinkade, remember you told me to keep my nose to the ground, that maybe I'd sniff out a story that'd tie in with the Christmas season?"

"Yep," the editor yawned, eyes refocused on the Macintosh monitor. "I remember."

"Chief, I think I've got *exactly* what you're

looking for!"

"Oh, really? Is that a fact?" the veteran newsman grunted.

"Yes, sir!"

"OK, Skip', suppose you let me in on this... scoop."

"I think you're gonna like it, Mr. Kinkade. It's got everything: it's seasonal, crammed with human interest, certain to mesmerize our readers, and it's--"

"Skip, how about getting to the point, will-ya? I'm a busy man."

"Sure, chief." Skipper told of the story circulating throughout Washington -- repeated from pulpits, in barber shops, restaurants, everywhere. Its gist was that a local blind street preacher had a revelation. In it, heaven instructed her to proclaim the coming of "A Miracle Baby" to be born in a DC ghetto and who'd rehabilitate Christmas.

When the reporter finished, Mr. Kinkade yawned, doused his cigarette in an overflowing ash tray and casually lit another. He then swiveled his chair and faced Skipper. "Son, how long you been working here?"

"Six weeks next Thursday."

"Sounds about right, kid. Lemme tell-ya something. I've been knocking around this newspaper for over twenty nine years -- a long time."

"Yes, sir."

"When you've circled the track as many times as I have, son, you see a lot of things come, lotta things go."

"I can imagine, sir."

"And trust me, stories like the kind you've stumbled on aren't worth one byte of space on your hard drive. Want you to listen to me. Ten years ago there was a jackleg preacher named Father Thorton. His church was in Southeast on Good Hope Road. Well anyway, Father Thorton had everybody in Washington all worked up over his prophesy that Armageddon would take place that year in DC, on the second Sunday after Easter, he said.

"Wisely, the *Post* didn't print that scoop. Anyway, the predicted day came and went -- a balmy one it was, not a cloud in the sky; people strolled in parks and enjoyed picnics. Armageddon failed to occur, just another lazy Sunday afternoon.

"Then, a couple of years later, there was Reverend Flapperstone. God told him, he boldly claimed, that the Washington Monument would dissolve into a puff of smoke at high noon on January eighth, and then the disciples Peter and John would appear in a rainbow over the capitol.

"Well, the Washington Monument is still standing down there on Constitution Avenue, and Peter and John, according to all evidence, remain in heaven. As for the prophetic preacher? Well, he died soon afterwards -- heart attack. Before passing, he assured his followers that on the third day he would rise and ascend into the heavens. The last time I heard, he was still in his grave, that is, if worms haven't snacked on him.

"Then, there was the preacher who called himself 'Prophet Vanderbelt.' Turns out the prophet part of his name shoulda' been spelled P-R-O-F-I-T. A first class chiseler he turned out to be. Anyway, he spread the word that--"

"Mr. Kinkade."

"Yes."

"I think I get the point."

"Good, Skipper, good. So I don't have to tell you I'm gonna have to pass on your Yuletide human interest story, do I?"

"No, sir," he sighed as he jammed his hands into his pants pockets.

"Happy to hear that, because though you may think I'm Old Man Scrooge himself, the truth is, I don't enjoy turning down a cub reporter's lead."

"I understand, sir."

"Wonderful. But, good try, Skip'."

"Thank you."

"Maybe next time."

"Yes, sir, maybe so."

After lighting another cigarette and coughing, Kinkade continued pecking away at his keyboard. He hated being interrupted -- especially by an eager beaver with a lead for a ridiculous story.

Weeks later, Mr. Kinkade was no longer the city editor. In fact, he wasn't an editor -- of *any* kind. Following a series of unprecedented events involving some people he'd never heard of, and wished he never had -- "Snake" Johnson, "Super," "Chicago Red," "Sweet Lucy." and a welfare couple, Willie and Louella Peterson -- the veteran newsman was demoted, nearly fired. He was reassigned a new office and given duties of dubious importance, one of which was proofreading classified ads. In his new office, a six-by-six broom closet -- "Hell's dungeon," colleagues called it -- he worked until his retirement. No gold watch for him, no going-away party either, and very few goodbyes.

By vetoing Skipper's "ridiculous" lead, Mr. Kinkade rejected what would have been the greatest Christmas feature in the *Post's* history -- and the most profitable. It was estimated the newspaper lost a half million dollars in advertising revenues by not running the story, plus a shot at winning the prestigious Edward R. Murrow Award for "excellence in journalism."

Defending his decision to anyone who'd listen -- no one at *The Post* did -- Mr. Kinkade said, "Now I ask you, how do you OK a story based on the words of some old blind street preacher claiming a 'wonder baby' born in a *ghetto* is going to save Christmas. Come on, give me a break!"

✽ *Chapter Six*

Outside the White House, freezing winds whistled. Inside, The President stood in the main corridor near the front portal.

"Gentlemen, are we ready?"

"Yes sir, Mr. President," a chorus of voices chimed.

The Chief Executive and his wife, followed by an entourage, stepped onto the portico. Before him, a sea of cameras clicked. Necks craned as spectators and reporters, jammed shoulder to shoulder, blanketed the lawn.

"Merry Christmas, everyone!" the President said, speaking into tiers of microphones.

"Merry Christmas, Mr. President!" thousands echoed.

From his notes the Chief Executive read what one journalist later termed "a few appropriate remarks." His aide then handed him a large switch whose chrome lever he snapped forward. "Click." The skyscraper of a Christmas tree fronting Sixteen

Hundred Pennsylvania Avenue ignited into a sparkling triangle.

With the presidential lighting of The Nation's Tree, the Christmas season officially began. It was Yuletide. Time for charity, fellowship and love. The season for reaffirming that it is more blessed to give than to receive.

This dictum Snake Johnson disagreed with. He liked to receive, that is, steal.

Several weeks before Christmas, Snake browsed an article in the *Washington Post* he "borrowed" from a doorstep. It reported that a local organization, Happy Youths At Yuletide (HYAT), had collected a large supply of toys donated by those wishing to "spread to underprivileged youngsters a little Christmas joy."

The charity planned to dole the playthings to needy children in response to their "Dear Santa letters." Snake saw the donations as an opportunity to join in the Christmas celebration with a little "receiving," then selling the toys.

The gifts, the article stated, were warehoused at Saint Jude's Church in the sixty thousand block of Wisconsin Avenue, just over the DC line in affluent Montgomery County, Maryland.

Contributions ("new, boxed toys only"), stated the article, would be accepted at the church, or arrangements could be made for pickup by dialing 301-555-GIFT during normal business hours. Snake, of course, planned to transact his "business" *after* normal business hours -- the darker the night the better.

He was certain the loot would be fence-able for at least six hundred dollars, maybe more -- "easy money." His scheme for acquiring the toys was simple -- burglarize the church and help himself. But to execute the plan, he'd need the help of his partner, "Super Six."

The following day, Snake sat at the kitchen table in Super's Southeast apartment. Idly he fingered a new Sony Walkman the host shoplifted the previous day. Shrugging, he set it aside. "This job, Sup'? Nothing to it, like picking a dead man's pockets."

"That easy, uh?"

"A breeze," he bragged.

Super frowned. "Look, ah, I don't know 'bout do'n' someth'n' like this, Snake, I mean, I'm on probation, I gotta be careful."

"Don't you think I know that?" Snake demanded, his voice rising.

"What I'm saying is, I don't believe the judge is gonna buy my 'I been converted' plea again. I'm good at acting, but I ain't that good. Besides, serious acting drains a man. Sure wouldn't wanna have to do it for a living. Frankly, I prefer our line of work."

"Same here, Sup'. Unlike with a regular job, we don't have to worry 'bout layoffs."

"Right on, brotha'. We got *real* job security. Only thing missing is health benefits."

"Well, guess you can't have everythin'," Snake shrugged.

"Got a point."

"Anyway, Sup', like I said, don't let this job

sweat-cha none. OK? We'll be in and outta that church before you can say 'Thank-ya, Jesus' three times. I figure we should be able to sell the toys for at least three big bills." Snake, of course, had six hundred dollars in mind, not three. "We'll split the take right down the middle. Fifty, fifty. Lemme see, if the selling price is three hundred, your cut'll be one hundred and twenty five," Snake said, aware Super wasn't very good at math -- even weaker in reading.

"You say my cut'd be a hundred and a quarter?"

"Guaranteed!"

"That sound 'bout right to me. OK, so count me in, partner."

"Welcome 'board."

"What's the plan?"

"Listen up."

A half hour later at Tony Lighthand's Quick Vehicle Rental, Snake and Super launched "Part One" of their "Master Plan." Flashing his disarming smile, Snake approached the clerk and presented "his" charge card, stolen, and "his" driver's license, which bore the name Antonio Debaldo Policiano. Snake rented the ID from "Slick" Morton, who also did a brisk business in renting stolen pistols and other people's identities.

"Ain't this a Eye-talian name?" the attendant asked, studying first the bogus ID, then Snake.

"Uh-huh."

"You don't look Eye-talian to me."

"Well, see it's like this. My great, great granddaddy, he was indentured. Anyway, he rented his services to 'Old Man' Policiano, an Italian plantation owner in Georgia. Great-great granddad liked the name so much he took it for his own."
"Oh. Sorry, I didn't mean to--"
"No problem," Snake grinned. "I get questions like that all the time."
"It's just that in this business you can't be too careful. We get a fake ID, I know, at least three times a week, more during the Christmas season."
"You're joking!" Antonio Debaldo Policiano exclaimed. "What *some* folks won't stoop to -- no principles at all."
"Got that right. Be nice if I only had to deal with honest customers like yourself, Mr. Policiano."
Mr. Policiano smiled. "You're so kind."
Fifteen minutes later, Super and Mr. Policiano sat in the cab of a new Ford station wagon, top of the line, complete with the L3-5 Luxury Package. Snake insisted on an upgraded vehicle. "If I don't get a wagon with that luxury package, you can forget my future business. And I *know* you don't want that."
"You got that right, Mr. Policiano."

✤ *Chapter Seven*

At around eleven-thirty that night, the ill-gotten station wagon quietly neared its destination. After switching off the headlights, Snake eased the vehicle to a stop a half block from Saint Jude's Church, then shut down the engine. He and Super looked around, scanning rows of manor-like homes and manicured lawns. The scene was like a snapshot from a postcard, serene, idyllic.

"Everything's looking real good, Sup'."

"Yeah. Don't see a soul. How 'bout you?"

"Same here."

"Ah, you ready?"

"Sure. Come on."

Snake released the hand brake, then, headlights still off, drifted the station wagon down the thoroughfare and into the church driveway. He parked near a side door. Again, both looked around. Darkness. Silence. From under his seat, Snake withdrew a crowbar, flashlight and two pairs of rubber gloves. They slipped on the gloves. Seconds later, both men stood in front of a side door. After Super pried its lock, they tiptoed inside. Snake flicked on the flashlight. "Click."

"This place look like some kinda, some kinda office, Snake."

"Yeah, do. Must be where the preacher work."

"Probably so. But where the toys, Snake, where the--"

"Newspaper said they in the basement."

"How we get there?"

"Beats me." They moved forward, several steps behind the flashlight's dancing beam. "Hey!" Snake whispered, "look!" They stopped.

"What?"

"Over yonder, to the left."

"Where? I don't see nothin.'"

"There...over yonder."

"Oh."

"See? It's a door."

"Yeah, I see. Come on, Snake. Maybe it go to the basement."

"Hope so."

Snake opened the door and the pair descended a flight of stairs leading to the basement, where, in its center, sat the toys, all boxed and neatly stacked.

Eying the loot, Super gloated. "Will-ya *look* at that, Snake, look at all them toys."

"I'm looking, partner, I'm looking."

"All them toys, Snake, just setting there, *waiting* for us to steal."

"Receive," the associate-thief corrected.

"Oh yeah, receive...whatever. Hey!" Super said.

"Huh?"

"Look at them envelopes taped to the boxes?"

"What 'bout' em?"

"What they for?"

"I don't know."

"Come on, let's find out."

They approached the boxes. From one, Snake removed an envelope, then ripped it open. Silently he read the letter that had been inside.

"*'Deer Mr. Sandda Cause,'*" it said, "*'my name is Jimmy Ragland. im sex, be seven soon. Momma sayed if i was good, you would bring me a Christmas toy. She sayed we to poor to buy any ourself. Said you need reel money to do that, not food stamps, which is all we ever have. by the end of the month tho, we don't even have them. Maybe if my daddee was here, he'd by me a Christmas toy. But daddee left long a go. Took everything. Cloes, shoes, raydeo, and a big part of me, my teacher said. The Christmas toy you bring is vary enportand. It might help me forget my daddy. For a while anyway.*

"*Momma sayed you must be proud of yoself and the work you do -- bringing children joy. Anyway, don't forget me this Christmas, the way you did last year. Momma told me to be sure to thank you. She sayed the world shore need more lik you, them that spred Christmas love and goodness.'*"

"What'd that paper say?" Super wanted to know.

"Ah, nothing. Just directions for putting the toy together," Snake lied.

"Oh. For a second, I thought it was something

important."

"Naw. Won't nothing."

"Hardly worth reading, uh?"

"Right, Sup', hardly worth reading."

Snake balled the letter and tossed it to the floor. Hurriedly unstacking boxes, both stepped on the sphere of paper several times. The crunching sound irritated Snake. He kicked the wad, landing it in a corner, conveniently out of the way -- and out of mind.

"Come on, we betta hurry up."

"Right."

In fewer than fifteen minutes, they filled the station wagon, then, exhausted, stood panting beside it.

"Want me to drive back, Snake?"

"Good idea." Both climbed into the vehicle. "Fine haul, uh?" Snake grinned, buckling his safety belt. "Fine."

"Betta believe it."

"Think of all that cash we gonna rake in for less than thirty minutes of our time."

"Sure beats working at McDonald's, don't it?"

"Who'd be dumb enough to work there for chump change?" They smiled as they looked smugly at each other. "Well, come on, let's get outta here."

"Yeah, this place make me nervous, reminds me that I'm still on probation."

Super switched on the ignition. "Vroom." The engine roared to life, revved, then, settled into a quiet purr.

Headlights off, the vehicle eased down the

driveway. As it pulled onto Wisconsin Avenue, Super spun the steering wheel, nosing south. A half block later, he flipped on the headlights.

"Told-ya, Sup', whole thing went off just like we planned."

"Sure did."

"E-e-e-a-sy payday."

"Any easier, we could stay at home and have'm mail the cash to us." Both chuckled.

Snow flurries began falling, dotting headlight beams with specks of whiteness. Super groped until he found the knob that turned on the windshield wipers, sighing in relief as they instantly responded: "swish...swish...swish...swish..." Soon, traffic slowed, first to a jog, then a crawl.

"Way them car's moving, gonna take us forever to get back," Super yawned.

"Sure look that way."

Snake, sighing, nestled into his seat. Now looking straight ahead, he saw ripple after ripple of blowing flakes. The two had loaded the toys nonstop. Snake was bushed, drowsy.

The windshield wipers arced hypnotically. "Swish...swish...swish...swish..."

As Snake listened to the wiper metronomes, his eyelids, now leaden shades, drooped. Gradually, they closed, transforming vision to darkness, which Snake probed, rummaging through memory; from it loomed the silhouette of a boy on a city sidewalk.

To the youngster's rear towered rows of tenements, wreaths on doors, frosted panes. Pedestrians wagged bags of presents. Near the corner, carolers sang: "Oh little town of Bethlehem, how still we..." Through the scene, a voice thrusted, ripping like a blade. "Robert! Robert!"

"I'm coming, Grandma Johnson."

"Hurry now."

"Yessum."

The skinny child skipped toward the corner tenement. He opened its door. In the hall, he stopped. His grandmother stood at the end of the corridor. He glanced at her, then stared. Something about her face was different. Ordinarily it was a sunbeam. Today her gentle, wrinkled face was a cloud, dark and somber.

"Grandma, are you alright? What's wrong? Is your rheumatism bothering you again?" No answer. "Ah, did momma stop by today, did she call?"

"Robert."

"Yes, m'am."

"Son, I want-cha to step back here to the kitchen with me. There's something I gotta tell-ya."

"Tell me?"

"Yes, so come on back."

"Yes, m'am."

She plodded into the room at the end of the hall. Robert hesitated, finally, he followed. "Have a seat, son." He sat at the kitchen table, she, at the opposite end. With sad eyes fixed on him, she sighed, "Robert."

"Yes, m'am."

"I don't know how to tell you this, and I really don't wanna have to tell you at all. But I gotta." Tightening, a tourniquet coiled her voice. "But whatever way I tell-ya, son, ain't gonna be easy or pretty for you...or me." Robert watched his grandma nervously finger the shawl draping her shoulders. "Guess there ain't but one way to do it -- just come right out with the truth." Following a graveyard-silent pause, she continued, "Robert."

"M'am?"

"Your momma ain't *never* comin' back to you no more."

Though he struggled to dam them, his eyes welled. "You mean, you mean, never?"

"Never. Listen, son, you old enough to know the truth. And the truth is, you never had no *real* mother to begin with, I mean, someone who was here when you needed her, to kiss-ya when you fell and hurt yourself, smothered you in her arms when you cried. Tell me, when was she *ever* in this house long enough to do any-a them things? You know the answer, well as me. Robert, what you had 'stead of a real mother was just someone who birthed you, nothing more.

"After she brought you in this world, she started running the streets, chasing this dream of hers, what she call 'the good life.' And what did the chase get her? The 'good life?' Naw. Life of a crack head, that's what -- some '*good life.*' During the past month, how many times have you seen her? I'll tell-ya. Twice. Then only for a flashing New York minute. After that, she was off again, like a shark chasing blood, still trying to find her...'good life.'"

"But Grandma, you don't really mean she ain't *never* com--"

"Son, listen, your momma phoned this morning, told me she and that no-'count 'Detroit Tony' got married last night. Detroit Tony, of all the slime on earth, why him? That man's the worst crook in DC, and sure to end up in the pen'tent'ary. Anyway, she said Detroit don't want no children, don't like'm, never did, 'specially somebody else's.

"He told her not to come over here and see you no more." She searched Robert's eyes. "Son, I don't enjoy bringing you news like this, but, like I said, you had to know sooner or later, you had to." She rose, plodded to his side and lowered her hands to his shoulders.

"Grandma, I--"

"And since you're learning the truth, you might as well hear it all." As if in excruciating pain, she closed her eyes. After finally unlocking them, she said, "Son, you know that money I been setting aside to buy your Christmas presents with?"

"Yes, m'am."

"Well, I ain't got it no more. Yesterday while you was in school and I was on my job, your momma stopped by here -- had to be her, she's the only one with a key -- and took it, every dime. Guess the monkey was riding'er, and she needed a hit. I'm sorry she stole your Christmas, son, won't fair, and just the thought of it sickens me to my heart."

Robert looked away. "When momma phoned did she say she wanted me to call her so she could say goodbye?"

"No."

"Didn't?"

"Uh-uh."

"Not even to say goodbye?"

"Not even that, son."

"You sure, Grandma?"

"Sure as God's on his mighty throne, Robert."

"It just don't seem right that she wouldn't want to at least say goodbye. I mean, to her own son."

"I know...I know..." The elderly Mrs. Johnson grimaced. "Robert, you gonna have to excuse me. My rheumatism's shooting pain through me like bullets. I gotta step upstairs and get my medication. Be right back."

"Yes, m'am."

The graying woman made her way down the hall, then mounted the stairs. By the time she reached the top landing, Robert had walked to the front door and opened it.

"Where you going, son?"

"Out."

"What for?"

"Just to walk, that's all."

"Where?"

"I don't know, Grandma. Just walk."

Feeling that the weight of the world was on his shoulders, he opened the door and headed down the steps. Stinging gusts whistled past. But strangely, he felt no pain. He walked to the corner. There, a quartet of carolers sang: "Mary had a baby...born in a manger...Mary had a..." With hands stuffed in his pockets, he ambled on. One block. Two. Three. How many? He had no idea. In what direction had he walked? He didn't know that either. Nor did he care.

"Momma, Momma!" Snake yelled, arms flailing, body thrashing, almost ripping his seat belt from its anchors. Super's eyes widened. The explosion of sound nearly startled him out of his skin. "Momma, please don't go, in the name-a God...don't...*don't* leave me!"

"What the hell's wrong with you?" Super frowned. "Snake, wake up, wake up!"

"Huh?"

Super nudged his troubled partner. "Hey! Hey! Come on, wake up!" He nudged his friend harder.

Snake opened his eyes and frantically looked around. "What happened? Where is she?"

"Where's who, Snake? Ain't nobody here but you and me. Come on, snap out of it!"

"What happened?"

"I don't know, Snake. You musta been dreaming. You was talking in your sleep."

"I was?"

"Yeah. Probably a nightmare. Way you was screaming and fighting, sounded like somebody was killing you."

Snake looked at his partner. "Sup'."

"What?"

"Somebody was."

Super studied Snake's eyes. The message in them was clear. His friend had exhumed something painful, something beyond discussion -- even with a friend.

"You alright now, Snake?"

"Yeah."

"You sure?"

"Uh-huh."

"That's good."

Super redirected his attention to the line of creeping cars in front of them.

"Where are we?" Snake wanted to know, wiping his eyes.

"Still on Wisconsin Avenue, 'bout a mile north of the District line."

"Sure ain't moved much, have we?"

"Naw. Traffic bit heavy tonight, people must be out celebratin'" The long procession of cars came to a stop. Stretching, Super stared at the glowing brake lights of the Toyota in front of them. "Ah, you mighty quiet, Snake."

"Yeah, I know."

"What-cha thinking?"

Snake shrugged. "Well, I was just...just setting here trying to figure out something, Sup', that's all."

"Oh? What?"

"Well, it's something that's been bugging me for a long time."

"Have, huh?"

"Yeah."

"You say 'a long time.' How long? Hours? Days? Months?"

"No, years."

"That *is* long. Tell me 'bout it."

"Sup', for all that time, I been trying my best to

figger something out. I've been asking myself over and over, is love...real. I mean, is there actually such a thing?"

"I'm pretty sure there is, Snake, gotta be. I mean, them smart folks write 'bout it, do it all the time. It's in the *Bible*, too. You know, love your neighbor, greater love has no man, stuff I learned in Sunday school -- few times I went. And they got love in movies, too. There's always lots-a kissing and touching, 'specially during the happy endings, with, you know, fiddle music, then the man and the woman hold hands, smile, hug, kiss. So I guess love's gotta be real and 'specially at Christmas time, Snake. That's when you hear ministers preaching 'bout it, that and fellowship and the Christmas spirit. And to show there really is a Christmas spirit and love, and that they got both, folks rush to department stores and charge tons-a stuff they can't afford, then give it to them they love, or...say they do."

"They sure do that at Christmas, alright. But you don't suppose the whole thing's just a, just a scam, do you?"

"What-cha mean?"

"You know, a trick by department stores, greeting card makers, Christmas tree sellers, and the like, to fool folks so they'll spend more and more money and make the sellers richer."

"Sure wouldn't surprise me none. Anyway, tell me, what do *you* think? Think there's really such a thing as love?"

"Ain't sure," Snake puzzled, scratching his

head. "Just ain't sure." He paused. "Sup'."
"Yeah."
"You ever had anybody love you? I mean,
really love you, just for who you is, knowing you
ain't nobody's saint."
"Um-m-m. That's a tough one," Super said,
pondering. "Gimme a little time, gonna have to think
about it. That ain't the kinda question a man can
answer instant."
After about a minute, Snake said, "Well, come
up with anybody?"
"Yeah, one person."
"Only one?"
"What-cha mean, only one? That was hard
'nough to do."
"Anyway, who was it?"
"My Aunt Wilma. And on second thought,"
Super added, "maybe I should say she *might* love
me."
"Why might?"
"Ah, come on, Snake, come on! You know how
people is. They're tricky, play games, grin in your
face, plant a knife in your back, all the while picking
your pockets. That's just the way us humans is
made. So I ain't even sure 'bout Aunt Wilma. She
claimed she loved me, but maybe she was lying
too."
"Good point. Like you say, folks is tricky."
"Don't I know it. Anyway, what about you,
Snake? You ever had anybody love you? I'm sure
you'll need time to think about it, right?"
"No."

"Oh? So what's the answer?"

Snake's painful reply was immediate. "I ain't *never* had nobody love me."

"Not ever, not even your momma?"

Staring at the line of motionless cars in front of them, Snake sighed, "'Specially not my momma, Sup'."

Super shrugged. "Well," he half smiled, "don't feel bad, Snake."

"What-cha mean?"

"Look at the good side. Leastwise, partner, you and me, we...we got each other, ain't we?"

"Yeah, Sup'...we got each other."

"Huh!" Super grunted, voice bristling with contempt. "All that talk 'bout love, charity and the Christmas spirit...bull! Who need that stuff anyway?"

"Yeah...right...who need it? "

✳ *Chapter Eight*

More exhausted than he'd ever been, Willie dragged into the dingy, rented room that was home. The pain in his back was intense.

"How'd your day go, hon?" Louella asked.

"It went, baby," he sighed, kissing her cheek, "...it went. And thank God it did, 'cause it was bitter cold out there!" He stepped to the rusty radiator and held his hands over it. "Sure ain't much heat coming outta this thing."

"Naw, hardly none."

"Would be nice if we could go to the landlord and complain."

"Yeah, would be, but how-ya do that when we're weeks behind in rent?"

"Right. So, I guess we'll have to live with a cold radiator and an even colder room." Willie, staring at the far wall, seemed vacuumed into dark thoughts. "Lou," he sighed, "what we're going through now, it ain't good, ain't good 'tall."

"I know, but still, Willie, we got a lot to be

grateful for. At least we have a roof over our heads. Some folks can't say that."

"That's for sure."

"By the way, where'd you park your cart?"

"In the back."

"Where exactly?"

"Near them ole junked cars."

"Oh. Hope nobody don't steal it. That cart's our meal ticket."

"Don't worry, Lou', I hid it under an ole raggedy mattress."

"Good thinking."

Now facing his beloved Louella, Willie, eyes alive with pride, suddenly beamed. "Lou'."

"Huh?"

"Got some good news for-ya."

"Do?"

"Yeah, had a *fine* day today. I collected 'nough cans to fill my cart three times, three *whole times.*" His smile brightened, then, as if shaded, it dimmed. "That's the good news, now the bad. The junk dealer said the price of aluminum dropped six cents a pound overnight."

"Now ain't that a crying shame, and after all your hard work, too."

"But, like I said, I filled my cart three times. Which ain't bad."

"How much did that bring?"

"Ten dollars." Willie spread two five dollar bills on the small table. "This oughtta help."

"Yeah, should. Ain't all we need, but every little bit count." She faced her husband. "Willie, to be

honest, I was beginning to wonder how we'd make
it to the end of the week. We down to our last can-a
soup. I warmed that for you, it's in that pan on the
stove."

"Thanks." Mid way to the small ancient stove,
Willie stopped. "Wait," he said, frowning. "Lou', if
you saved the soup for me, what'd *you* have to
eat?"

"Couple slices of bread. I scraped the mold off
real good."

"You should-a eat the soup, Lou'. You're the
one pregnant, not me. So you should-a eat it, baby."

"Willie, knowing you was out there in that
freezing weather, I was sure you'd be starving."

"No, Louella, no!"

"You mean you ain't hungry, Willie?"

"Don't mean that: I mean *you're* the one who's
gonna eat the soup. That's what I mean."

"But--"

"And don't try to talk me out of it, neither,
'cause I ain't listening."

Before she could voice further objections, Willie
stepped to the kitchen area at the end of their room
and opened a cabinet to fetch a bowl. Startled by the
explosion of light, a big cockroach raced across the
shelf -- a streaking dot of mahogany swift as thought.
Instantly, Willie's palm raked the intruder.
"Got'm!" The pest, wings flapping, flittered down,
landing near Louella.

"Oh, my!" she screamed, "Willie, Willie, get
that nasty thing outta here!"

"Don't worry, I'll get'm. Hold on, I'll get the

dirty little..."

Eyes fixed on the speeding speck, he scurried to her side. "Willie! Willie! Can't you do something? Please do something. I hate them things!"

Willie stood over the insect and, raising his foot, cocked it. The cockroach streaked to the left, right, momentarily stopped, then, darting, it reversed directions. Willie's foot fired. "Bam!" Floorboards trembled. The tiny table vibrated, a salt shaker on it toppled, crash landing in a chair, and spinning, dropped to the floor. From under Willie's shoe, a brownish liquid squirted --"squish!"-- splattering the leg of Louella's chair.

"Oh merciful heavens!" she squealed. "Will-ya look at that awful stuff. Just look at that mess! Ever see anything so *nasty* in all your life?"

"Relax, Lou', *relax*, it's gonna be alright, gonna be alright, be fine."

"And Willie, they come in here every day through them cracks, like soldiers on patrol."

Willie circled his arm around his wife. "Listen, Lou'," he said, "lemme tell-ya something. It really hurt my pride for you have to live this way, especially at Christmas, when you and me, we should be thinking 'bout *good* times, enjoying good things, not *this*. A roach farm ain't no place for my wife, especially when she pregnant. Knowing you have to live in all-a this, make me feel bad, baby. I don't know how to say it. I really don't. To tell-ya the God-in heaven truth, it make me feel like I'm *half* a man, *less* a husband, and don't deserve to be no father at all."

Looking at her husband with eyes of love, Louella reached up to touch his cheek. "Willie, I know you're doing the best you can. No wife could ask for more."

"But still, Lou', I..."

"Times'll change. There will be betta days, betta Christmases, too." She slipped her hand into his. The softness of her touch soothed. "I understand what you must be going through, Willie. Trust me, I do." Lowering, he nestled his face against her breasts. The mounds of flesh tranquilized. Soon, his tempest calmed.

He wiped the cockroach residue from the chair's leg and after washing his hands and the bowl, now filled with soup, he approached Louella. "Here."

"No, Willie, I want you to have it."

"I can't eat it, Lou'. Understand? I *can't*."

"But..."

He lowered the plastic container. "Go on now, baby, take it," he gently said. She looked up, then hurriedly clasped the vessel, tilting it to her lips. Later, she handed him an empty bowl and watched as he walked to the sink. "By the way," he said, washing the container, "the landlord, did he stop by today?"

"Been doing that off and on for nearly three weeks."

"What'd he have to say?"

"The usual, that he sympathized and want to work with us long as he can, but that he can't do much more. Just *can't.*"

"Um."

"Told me he has mortgage notes to pay, and that they're coming due soon."

"Well, guess, like us, he got money problems too." Willie set the clean bowl in the cabinet and stared at it. Louella sensed he was retreating into dusky introspection. "Lou'," he sighed.

"Yeah."

"I wonder how this whole thing's gonna turn out. I just wonder." He turned to face her.

Sensing his mood, Louella realized it was time to change subjects. "Ah, Willie, tell me, that old blind preacher woman you talk 'bout."

"Blind Reverend Mary?"

"Right. You seen her lately?"

"Yeah, yesterday, while I was going through some trash bins near Rhode Island and Florida Avenue."

"Has she talked to you since the last time you mentioned her?"

"Naw. Usually when I see'r now, I'm a ways away."

"Can you hear her preaching from where you are?"

"Most of the things she say, yeah."

"Is she still making the same prophesy 'bout our baby?"

"The very same, still talking 'bout the coming of the Miracle Child. And she say the time will be 'soon.'"

"Well, Willie, if, like she say, our child's gonna

change Christmas and people's hearts, with so much hate and greed everywhere this holiday, his birth sure can't come none too soon."

"That's for sure, Lou'."

A couple of hours later, both lay in bed.

"Willie," Louella said, "I was thinking 'bout this just today. You know, during Christmas back home in Virginia, we always put up some kinda decorations."

"Yeah, we did."

"Won't much, but we put it up. But this year we ain't put up a thing, not nothing to remind us it's the season of good will and love. Was thinking we oughtta put up, you know, *something*."

"I agree, but we can't afford stuff like that, Lou'. Fact, a few days ago, a fella selling Christmas trees tried to interest me in one -- giveaway prices, too. 'Course I couldn't buy it."

"That goes without saying. But I was thinking the decoration don't have to be nothing fancy or expensive, Willie."

"What-cha got in mind?"

"Oh-h-h-h, I don't know. Maybe some ole wrapping paper somebody throwed away, or a Christmas card you find in the trash. We could cross out the name. Things like that."

"Oh," Willie said. "Just thought, there's a woman who live off Florida Avenue; she got lots of evergreens in her back yard. Maybe she'll gimme one or two little twigs."

"That'd be good. We could tack'em to the door, hang some in the window." She slowly turned her pregnant frame so she could face him. "Willie, tell me something."

"What?"

"With all our problems -- you know, your busted back, rent overdue, little food -- with all-a that, think you got the Christmas spirit this year?"

"Lou', having you as my wife, 'course I got it, and because you *is* my wife, I keep it all year long."

"Willie," she said, fighting back the tears, that was a thoughtful thing to say."

"Just telling the truth, Lou', just telling the truth."

She turned her back to the man she loved, hoping he wouldn't see her cry. She was afraid if he did, he might mistakenly think she was shedding tears of sadness. She wasn't.

✳ *Chapter Nine*

Several blocks east of where Willie and Louella lay sleeping, "Big Daddy" Washington squeezed his three hundred-pound-plus frame into a booth at his all-night diner, Big's Food Heaven.

Having accomplished this remarkable feat, he sorted through a fistful of policy slips, checking, as he did daily, to see if any player on his books had a "hit."

Though sometimes grudgingly, especially if the payoff were a large one, Big never welshed on a bet. "Man's gotta have honor and integrity, ya know," the large lawbreaker often philosophized to any one who'd listen.

Honor was something Big also demanded from those he did business with. Last summer he didn't get it from "Speedy," his former numbers runner who shortchanged him out of three hundred dollars. Speedy spent nine days in intensive care -- compliments of Big and a baseball bat.

The front door of the diner swung open.

Grinning, Snake and Super strode in. Both carried considerable cash. An hour earlier, their fence, "Tricky Dick," gave Snake six hundred dollars for the stolen toys. Snake told his partner he'd only received two hundred, so Super's "half share," according to Snake's math, was reduced to seventy-five dollars.

"Like I say, good buddy, split right down the middle. Satisfied?"

"Couldn't be more!" replied his trusty friend.

"Pleasure doing business with you!"

"Same here, partner."

Super and his companion came to the diner to celebrate their coup by feasting on a large, first class meal -- "best in the house."

"What's happening, Big Daddy?" Snake grinned as he and Super stood beside the proprietor.

"Nothing," Big frowned, "'except I just found out somebody hit on my books for five thousand bills."

"Smile, Big. It's Christmas time, time, they say, for sharing with your fellow man."

"Yeah, but they ain't the one gonna have to shell out the five thousand."

"Come on, Big, get into the season's spirit," Snake chuckled.

Pouting, Big was as silent as tomb.

"Martha!" Snake bubbled, turning to the waitress who was placing a Blue Plate Special on a customer's table. "Martha, baby."

"Yeah."

"I want nothing but first class for me and my

business associate here. *First class.* Understand?"

"First class, uh?" Martha yawned. "I guess you mean The Blue Plate Special, right?"

"I'm insulted! The Blue Plate Special? That's for your *common* sort. Martha, you're looking at men of means."

"That's mighty big talk, Snake. Sure hope you men *of means* can pay for what you order."

"Chump change, chump *change!* Right partner?" Super smiled in agreement. "But 'nough small talk. Look, got any them big Grade A, juicy T-bones back there in the kitchen?"

"Probably more'n you can pay for."

"How 'bout bringing us a couple, will-ya, with side orders of top quality fresh peas and your *best* made-from-scratch potato salad*?* And oh yeah, a couple bowls of that Golden Supreme All Natural Ice Cream, none-a that cheap, artificial stuff. See, Martha, me and my business partner here, we just closed a big Christmas transaction up in rich Montgomery Country -- spreading Yuletide spirit while turning a profit. Private enterprise at its best, the *American way.*"

"Big Christmas deal, uh?" Martha stood with hands fisted on her wide hips.

"You heard right. By the way, Martha," Snake said, winking at Super.

"Yeah."

"Did I forget to mention the four dollar tip we plan to leave-ya? That's four a piece. A little Christmas love for-ya."

"Eight dollars!" Martha exclaimed, now

energized. "Ah, excuse me, sir," she said to the customer she was serving, "you gonna have to wait. Charley!" she yelled to the cook, "double Ts, salad-tat, best peas, ice, Prem'. And Charley, *executive express!*" Hurriedly she disappeared into the kitchen where she and the other waitress, Sheretta, bickered.

"Eight dollars?" Sheretta gasped. "They're at my table and you *know* it."

"*Like hell!*" Martha hissed.

Seeing the unrest he'd instigated, Snake chuckled. After he and Super sat, he flipped out a Camel and lit it. "'That job tonight, was a blowout, won't it, Sup'?"

"Right on. Ah, got any ideas for our next hit?"

"What-cha mean, 'next'? Thought you was worried about violating your probation?"

"I was, but this money tonight came so *easy* and looked so *good*. Anyway, got anything else lined up?"

"Not off the top of my head, no. But who knows, I might come up with something."

"Sure hope so."

Later, Martha reappeared and placed the orders in front of 'the men of means.' "Ah, them steaks, they cooked to the satisfaction of you gentlemen?" she wanted to know.

With a fork, Snake probed and jabbed his. "Yeah, Martha, mine's just right."

"Same here," Super agreed.

"Good, good," Martha smiled, then left. Less than ten seconds later, she reappeared. "Everything alright?"

"Ah, yeah," Snake frowned, "everything's fine, just fine." Martha continued to loiter. "Martha."

"Yeah, Snake, ah, I mean, yes, *sir,* Mr..."

"How 'bout leaving us the hell alone, will-ya? We business men, got big deals to discuss." He waved her away with his fork. "We talking confidential matters here. Can't have you eavesdropping, then selling our secrets to the competition."

Shrugging, Martha stomped off.

After eating his steak, Super said, "Snake, just thought-a something."

"What?"

"Something that could be our next job."

"What-cha got in mind?"

"Well, there's this old blind woman, a street preacher, Blind Reverend Mary Sweetwater. Maybe you've seen'er. She preach in that vacant lot on Florida Avenue."

"Yeah, I've passed her a few times."

"Anyway, she--"

"Wait a minute, Sup', now don't set there and tell me you've come up with some nickel and dime scheme to mug a blind woman for maybe three bucks -- or less. If so, count me out -- ain't worth my time."

"Snake, this ain't no small time operation. Folks tell me that woman's got *all kinds-a money.*"

"Who told you that?"

"Crap, Two Pound, JT and Big Al, too."

"You *sure* you got this story straight?"

"'Course. Heard'em talking 'bout it with my

own ears, over at the pool hall."

"Did, uh? Um-m-m. Sound like you might be on to something, partner."

"I know I am."

"Where she stash the money? In a bank? If so, I can flimflam her into withdrawing it, Sup'. No problem."

"Naw, she don't keep it there. Crap said she don't trust banks."

"So where she keep it?"

"Word on the street is, it's hidden in that room she rent."

"Um-m-m-m. At *her* place, uh? That do make it mighty convenient. Ah, where she live?"

"In one-a them tenements near the old Freedman's Hospital."

"*There, you say?* Look, Sup', if she live there, maybe we barking up the wrong tree after all."

"What-cha mean?"

"Use your head, Sup'. Anybody renting a crummy room in that neighborhood don't have no money -- *serious* money, the kind worth stealing. Ah, I mean, *receiving.* Folks with big bucks got homes on upper Sixteenth Street, or near Rock Creek Park, places like that."

"Look, Snake, you don't understand. They tell me that old broad's the kind that save everything, *every dime.* You know the type. She probably live there to skimp on rent, so she can add to her fortunes. Like I said, you know the type."

"True. I've met her kind. Well, not exactly met, but visited their homes when they weren't there."

Snake smiled. "You understand what I mean?"

"'Course. Anyway, that's the kind-a woman she is, a *saver*. And they say she's been saving money for years."

"Um, this thing's beginning to sound more and more interesting."

Martha reappeared and once again loitered near the diners. "Everything alright?"

"Look, Martha!" Snake said, fumbling for his wallet. "Here's your tip. He plucked four one dollar bills from his billfold and after collecting an equal amount from Super, unfolded the gratuity across Martha's burning palm. "Now, Martha, will you *kindly* leave us alone? Like I told-ya, we got big deals to discuss, don't wanna be disturbed. Understand?"

The waitress counted the bills several times to be sure they were all there and were legal tender. She then slipped the gratuity into her apron pocket. Nearby, Sharetta glared at the coworker who'd "stolen" her customers. "I still say that was *my* table!" she bristled

"I ain't stole nothing!" Martha shot back.

"Now y'all stop all that squabbling back there!" Big Daddy growled, his jowls flapping. "This here's Christmas time, customers came here to enjoy a holiday meal, not listen to The Third World War. So cut it out!"

"Yessuh," Sharetta mumbled, scowling at Martha as both antagonists withdrew to the kitchen.

"Ah, now where was we, Sup'?" Snake said.

"I was telling you where the old woman stashed

all them thousands, no, *millions*."

"Right, you was."

"See, I figure it this way. You and me, we can break in and--"

"Break in?" Snake interrupted. "Not on a job like *this*, Sup'! Why break in when you can con the woman into *inviting* you in? Get it?"

"Um, never thought-a that."

"Sup', if you gonna work with me, you gotta think big time, *professional*. Anyway, once you're invited in, you can search everywhere. She can't see nothing: you can rob her blind."

"Rob her blind. Hey, that there's a good one, Snake." Super grinned. "Rob her blind. So when we gone pull this thing off?"

"What-cha mean we?"

"Me and you."

"Not we, Sup', but me."

"Ah--"

"Look, let's face it, I got a natural talent for conning."

"It's a gift from God alright. Well," Super grinned with a shrug, then added, "maybe *not* from God, but it *is* a gift."

"Right. The way I see it, I'll con my way into the old woman's place, OK? And then I'll--"

"But what about me, Snake?"

"Don't you fret. I'll split the take -- fifty fifty, just like we did tonight. After all, the idea was yours. So, you're entitled to a consultant fee."

"What's a consultant?"

"Ah, it's somebody who dreams up a heist, but

don't take part in it, yet split the take down the middle. Understand?"

"I think I do."

"For you, Sup', that's close 'nough."

"By the way."

"What?"

"Word on the street is this old preacher claim she had a vision. She said a voice told her some *miracle baby* was gonna be born in a rundown neighborhood right here in DC, and that he'd re...re...rehabilitate Christmas,' -- whatever that mean -- and change folks' hearts."

"She said that?"

"So they tell me."

"This crazy story she spreading," Snake asked, stroking his chin, "ah, is people buying it?"

"All the way. Some say they can't wait for the birth, that maybe then we'd have a betta world."

"Interesting. Could be her prediction can bring us a few *extra* bucks."

"How?"

"Too complicated to explain," Snake replied. "You'll have to trust me on this one."

"If you say so, partner."

Later, as the pair walked towards the door, Martha, who stood near a rear booth, smiled. "Ah, thanks for the Christmas gift, gentlemen."

"No big thing," Snake grinned. "It's Yuletide, baby, time for love and sharing."

"Snake, ah, I mean, Mr. Johnson, the world sure need more like you, folks with love in their heart for their fellow man -- and woman."

"Martha," Snake grinned, "I'm flattered. Like, what can I say? Except that I do the best I can to spread goodness during the holy season, just like the *Bible* teach."

"You sure do that. And, God bless-ya. Oh, by the way, Snake, I hope you have a prosperous holiday."

"I got a feeling I will, Martha. "Fact, I'm *sure* I will." He elbowed his buddy in the ribs and chuckled. "Right, Sup'?"

"Right on, partner," Super grinned ear to ear, "...*right on!*"

✳ *Chapter Ten*

The following day Blind Mary, as usual, preached in her vacant-lot church. Several men gathered before her. Among them was one Robert Snake Johnson. Most in the congregation had come for spiritual enrichment. Snake was not one of them. He was there for enrichment, alright, but *not* the spiritual kind.

When Mary's service ended, he approached her.

"Excellent sermon!" Snake bubbled. "I never heard a better one!"

"How kind of you."

"And that's from a man who's been a churchgoer for *years*, so I've heard some of the best."

"Good. Ah, tell me, young man, which church do you attend?"

"Ah, I don't mean I attended churches here in Washington, you understand." The only churches Snake ever set foot in were those whose ministers asked him to leave. "See, I only recent moved to the

city. I meant churches in a little town in North
Carolina, where I was born -- Bunn.   You ain't
never been there, have you?"
    "No."
    "That's *good.*"
    "Good?"
    "I mean, ah, it's good a *fine* lady like yourself
ain't been exposed to the serious poverty in Mon --
terrible place."
    "Oh."
    "Anyway, like I said, I've heard many a
sermon, but not one can equal yours."
    "Thank you. By the way, young man, you say
you're a churchgoer, but have you been *saved?*"
    "'*Course!* Baptized at eleven, in Gethsemane
Baptist Church in Bunn. It was indeed a uplifting
experience, uplifting!"
    "Happy to hear that."
    "Ain't it strange how a body *never* forget the
age he was when he saw the light?"
    "Yes, it is."
    "Being a better than average student of the
Good Book myself, I can certainly tell you know a
lot 'bout the *Bible.* In my case, sadly, I don't read
the scripture like I used to -- eyes getting bad. But I
do enjoy learning from them who truly know and
understand The Word. So I was wondering if you'd
be kind enough to share a few minutes of your time
and *Bible* knowledge with me, so you can teach
me?"
    "Be happy to, son."
    "Now ain't that nice. And I do 'preciate it.

What-cha say we have our lessons over some refreshments at a McDonald's?"

"Good idea."

"Wonderful, wonderful," the Bible student said.

"Ah, you ready, Rev'?"

"Anytime."

Snake escorted his patsy around the corner to a McDonald's.

"What'll you have?" he smiled, assisting Mary into a booth.

"Coffee'll do nicely. Cream and sugar."

"How many of each?"

"One."

"Be right back."

Snake soon returned with two cups of coffee and placed them on the table. He then sat opposite Mary, watching as she put sugar and cream into her cup.

"Hope-ya enjoy the refreshment, Rev'."

"Yes, thanks."

The con man studied his target, wondering if the deception used thus far was working. Seemingly it was. Mary contentedly sipped from her cup, her demeanor suggesting she had been gullible to her student's every word.

"Rev', I 'preciate you taking your time to teach me about The Good Book. But let me say, I ain't exactly a dummy on the subject to begin with. For example, right off the top-a my head, I can name all the Disciples. Lemme see, there was John Peter and Matthew Thomas and--"

"No, son. That's Peter and John, Matthew and

Thomas."
  "Oh, yeah, you right. Ah...funny how when
your eyesight's fading like mine, and you can't see
words too clear on the page, names sorta get
jumbled. But thank goodness, I got you here to help
me."
  "My pleasure."
  Snake's attention wasn't fully focused on his
lesson, but on the blind woman's money. He
wondered where she hid it: under her bed, in a
mattress, a trunk, taped to the underside of a table
top, etc. Certain the take would be a king's treasure,
he could scarcely contain himself. He could scarcely
wait to curl his fingers around Mary's fortune, every
dime.
  As he eyed the victim, he envisioned himself,
now sinfully rich with her money, cruising down
Seventh Street, encircled in the lushness of a fully-
accessorized convertible -- fire engine red. The classy
road machine was a showroom-new Mercedes. Its
top was down. His hands draped the steering wheel,
chin angled just so -- perfect profile.
  Accompanying him were several *Vogue* model-
types, youthful, vibrant all with windblown hair,
three in the back seat, one in the front. Each
competed to touch any part of his exquisite body, or
anything covering it: like his fine French-tailored
trousers, silk shirt, hand stitched loafers, anything.
On the sidewalk, rows of admirers gawked at their
icon.
  "Ain't that Snake Johnson?"
  "Snake? You mean...*Mr. Robert Johnson!*"

"Local boy makes good."

"Yeah, *Mr. Big Time himself.*"

Soon a motorcycle policeman approached the Mercedes and signaled its driver to pull over. Violation? Impeding traffic, driving three miles an hour in a thirty miles an hour zone. The young cop dismounted. Approaching, he suddenly recognized the celebrated motorist.

"Ah, ah, it's you, Mr. Johnson. I didn't know, sir. Where-ya headed?"

"To The Rich-Only Club in Georgetown."

"Yes, sir." Flipping on its siren, the officer whirled his motorcycle to the front of the Mercedes and led the man of means to his destination.

"And it is written," Blind Mary said, lowering her cup, "that those who worship earthly vanities are doomed to hell's grief." She paused, then asked. "Do you believe that, son?"

"Huh?" the Mercedes owner said, startled from his fantasy.

Mary repeated the admonition. "And I was wondering if you believe that."

"Believe it? Why, that's like asking if I honor the teachings of the *Bible*. Why 'course I believe it."

"That's good, son."

Snake wondered how the old woman could be so cruel. Why would she nose dive his fantasy, especially when it was nearing "the good part?"

An hour later Snake said, "Ah, look, Rev', if you don't mind I'd like to have the honor of escorting you to your place. And I won't take no for a answer," he chuckled.

"Walk me home? No, Robert, that won't be necessary."

"Rev', it's my *moral* duty to escort you. Why it's the least I can do to show 'preciation for all the *Bible* you've taught me."

"Son, surely you must have better things to do with your time."

"Reverend, let me remind you there are *bad* people out here, 'specially at Christmas time: muggers, *con men*, folks, unlike myself, who look on The Fourteen Commandments as a joke."

"That's the Ten Commandments," Mary corrected.

"Of course. But ten or fourteen, the point is, a blind lady like yourself is in danger walking alone on these mean streets."

"I--"

"Even me, a man, I don't feel safe 'round here. Never can tell when you're gonna run across some *bad* person."

Mary finally consented to the Good Samaritan's offer. They left and as they walked, Snake raised question after question about the Bible and philosophy. His purpose was to keep the old woman talking, keep her mind occupied. That way, she wouldn't have time to consider the wisdom of allowing him, a total stranger, to escort her to where she hid the treasure.

"Rev', do you think aborted babies go to heaven?"

She did.

"Is there a place in Paradise for the rich?"

"Yes, provided they haven't tainted their souls in acquiring wealth."

"What race was Christ?" Snake asked.

"All and none. He is the embodiment of *every* man, race, nationality, and culture. He encompasses *all* humanity, born and unborn, yet He retains heavenly perfection."

"As a holiday, what do you think of Christmas, Rev'?"

"It is a time for reaffirming the search for love, without which man is hollow. Each Yuletide he renews that search, hoping to recapture love's essence. For love is as essential as air. Without it, man is nothing."

When they reached Mary's rooming house, Snake said, "Reverend, your teachings is getting more and more interesting. Really hate to stop my lesson. Ah, why don't I just step up to your room and you can go on instructing me? 'Cause heaven as my witness, I *really* wanna learn. Know what I mean?"

"I think I do."

"Good. So why don't I just go inside with you? Be safer for-ya that way, 'cause a body can't tell who'll be lurking in hall shadows, waiting to mug him -- or her."

"Son, fear is not a word I know. Every day I walk through valleys of shadows. But the hand of God shields me."

"Reverend, what I'm saying is--"

"But, if you'd like to step up to my room so we

can learn together, I have no objections."

Snake grinned. "Your allowing me go to your room with you make me the happiest man on earth. Believe me. *The happiest.*"

The first thing Snake did when he entered Mary's room was to case it. Her living quarters were simple, unpretentious. A veteran dining table sat in front of the window. On it rested a Bible. Flanking the table were two oak chairs. Though serviceable, both showed their age. An easy chair angled the far corner. Fronting it was a little stool, the upholstery worn. A chest of drawers, shoe boxes stacked under it, sat near the radiator. Layer upon layer of faded varnish coated the antique storage piece. Her narrow bed, an old army cot, butted the far wall.

After helping the preacher into the easy chair, Snake sat on the stool in front of her.

"Fine place you got here."

"Well, it meets the needs of an old blind woman whose wants are modest."

"'Course...'course it do."

Snake wanted Mary to continue talking. The more she talked, the better, making it easier for him to search the room. He raised additional theological and Biblical questions. Patiently she responded.

As she monologued, he quietly slipped off his shoes. "Now ain't that the gospel truth?" he said after Mary quoted a Biblical passage. As she talked on, he tiptoed to the bureau. The top drawer he eased open and rummaged through it. Inside, nothing. Nothing of value, that is: a little teddy bear, a doll with a broken arm, two blouses, an equal number of skirts.

"And the Good Book teaches the reason for the Christmas season in *John 3:16...*" the preacher went on, apparently unaware Snake was now on all fours and looking under the bureau.

With eyes fastened on her, he slowly and quietly slid out one of the shoe boxes stored there and removed its lid. It housed a few socks and several pieces of worthless costume jewelry. *Damn!* What a waste of his time! He silently rummaged through the remaining boxes. In the second was a pair of tattered bedroom slippers. The third, stacks of old letters, all yellowed -- another zero. Where did she stash the *money?* Where? He was about to replace the lid on the box of letters when the one on top caught his eye. He picked it up, unfolded it.

"'*Dear God,*'" he read, "*as the oncoming blindness dims my sight. But I do not despair. Failing vision, I am learning, is like a Christmas gift. For though my eyes dim, my insight grows brighter. And now I see goodness I never saw before, in the darkest of hearts and the darkest of places. Wiser, I learn to practice what you taught: to love and forgive all, even those who victimize me for greedy ends. And so, Father, I remain your humble servant, with failing sight, but greater vision. Mary.'*"

Snake refolded the letter and returned it to the box. He decided not to read another. Why waste time? The others, he was sure, would be just as stupid as the one he'd read, containing not a word about where the money was hidden. What the old woman had written was foolish -- her loss of eyesight, *a gift*; without eyes, able to see with greater vision. *Crap!* He had come for money, not to read *stupidity.* Where was the loot?

He replaced the lid, opened another box and fingered through it. Inside were spools of thread, balls of yarn, and a few knitting needles of various colors and sizes. Hell! Another strikeout.

"The ways of heaven are beyond our understanding," Mary said, talking to an empty stool. Snake tiptoed back to the stool and sat.

"That it is, Rev'. And so we question the judgment of Providence."

"Indeed we do, knowing not His wisdom or timetable."

"Amen...amen."

As Mary talked on, Snake sneaked back to the bureau and rummaged through the third and fourth drawers. Results? More of the same: nothing of value. Thus far, not a single coin, *not one*, let alone the king's ransom he envisioned. Mary continued discoursing with herself. Then, abruptly, in the middle of a sentence, she stopped. Silence crashed like a lead pipe on a tin roof.

Snake froze. He wondered why the old woman stopped talking? Leaning forward, he stared at her. She seemed to stare back. But how could that be? She was blind. Squinting, he focused on her eyes -- as before, they were a pair of lifeless blanks. Still, she was *looking* at him, he knew it.

"Son," Mary said, "I want you to come back over here, hear me?"

The words startled him. How could she know he wasn't sitting in front of her? Snake quickly returned to the stool and sat. "Rev', I've been right here all 'long."

"Have you?"

"'Course. Anyway, you blind, how you know *where* I was?"

"Knowing that has little to do with sight, son. But everything to do with vision. You can know what's in the heart without having eyes, and the heart, that's where I look. The fact is, having eyes is often an obstacle to *seeing*. Son, listen, from the moment you started talking to me on that vacant lot, I *saw* you clearly."

"Rev', to be honest, I ain't sure I understand what you're talking 'bout"

"You can stop the acting now, son. It's no longer necessary."

"Acting? Who's acting? What-cha mean?"

"Robert, I want you to listen to me."

"Ain't I been doing that all 'long?"

"No. Moving about the room the way you were, you heard, but you never listened. Now, I want you to listen. Because if you do, I can save you a lot of time and energy, so you won't have to continue frustrating yourself."

She paused. "You're not going to find what you came looking for, Robert. You see, it's not here -- at least, not the kind of riches you have in mind. Son, if you came searching for some great sum of money, you'll be disappointed. My only treasure is the gold of charity I feel for others -- *you*, Robert, included. That wealth I share, gladly. Plus, if you see anything in the room you want, *it's yours.*"

"Rev', I--"

"Don't rush, look around. Take anything your heart desires. And oh yes, before I forget, you'll find about forty dollars and change in that baking powder can on the sink counter -- my grocery money. I apologize that it's not much, but it's all I have to offer. But, it's yours for the taking."

Snake was dumbfounded. Her words jolted, impaling like a stake. He stared at the blind preacher; his mouth gaped, jaw dangled. What the woman said he couldn't believe he heard -- an invitation to freely help himself to what he'd come to steal. "Rev', I ain't never in my life met *nobody* like you, never."

"And, son, if you take something, don't worry: I won't call the police after you're gone and report it stolen."

"I...I...don't know what to say."

"You don't?"

"No, m'am."

"Maybe I can help. You might start by telling the truth about yourself. The *real* truth, not yarns about bad eyesight to explain your inability to read the Good Book, and no more of that talk about being a faithful churchgoer. This time, try the truth, son. Trust me, it works." She smiled. "And don't worry, Robert, these old ears can handle the truth, regardless of how ugly it might be."

Snake scratched his head. "You mean, you mean you really wanna hear 'bout somebody like *me*? Snake Johnson?"

"Why, of course."

"You sure you want that, Reverend?"

"Sure as I'm blind."

"Lady, ain't *nobody* never wanted to hear nothing 'bout me. Folks never cared, one way or another -- my momma included. See, they know what kinda person I am."

"Well, I'm not 'they,' son, I'm me. I love everyone equally, just as our Heavenly Father does. I care, Robert. So why don't you start by telling where you were really born?"

Snake lowered his head...and voice. "I was born right here," he mumbled, "in DC. Over in them projects."

"So, it wasn't in Bunn, North Carolina, after all?"

"No, m'am, weren't, but in the Southeast Projects."

"From what I hear, that neighborhood is one *fearful...awful...place.*"

"You sure heard right."

"Ah, tell me about your father."

"I can't."

"Why?"

"Don't know that much 'bout him. Only seen'm a couple of times."

"Oh."

"And that was long ago. First meeting lasted 'bout ten minutes, second less. Today I wouldn't recognize the man. He could be any stranger I pass on the street."

"I see," she sighed with sadness.

Snake spoke of his mother, but only passingly. He told of how she deserted him one Christmas, never returning. "And," he added, "since you say you want the truth, *all* of it, there's something else you oughtta know. I've been jailed, I mean, incarcerated."

"Once?"

"*Many* times."

"How many?"

"I lost count."

"What charges?"

"'Bout every thing you can name, except murder." Snake lowered his eyes, studied the floor, then looked at Mary. "Well?" he said, waiting for her reaction. She gave none. "Well?"

"Well what?"

"I thought by now you'd be threatening to call the police or ordering me to leave."

"You're welcome here, son."

"Is my ears hearing right?"

"They are."

"You mean, you mean you ain't gonna call the cops?"

"No."

"Look, ah, knowing what you now know 'bout me, ain't-cha *scared* of what I might do?"

"Not in the least."

"When folks learn 'bout the mean things I've done, and I've done some rotten ones, they usually get jittery."

"Do they?"

"Very."

"Take a good look at me, Robert."

"I am."

"Do I look jittery?"

"Ah, no, m'am, not even a little."

"Son."

"Yes, m'am," he whispered.

"I want you to come closer to me."

Snake's eyes widened. "Closer?" he puzzled.

"Yes."

"Ah..." Like a steel band, uncertainty choked his voice. "Why?"

"Being close to me, son, does that bother you any?" Snake didn't answer, nor did he make an attempt to move. "Look, I'm just an old blind woman. What possible harm could I do to you, a big...strong...man?"

"I..." Finally he inched forward, then stopped. "How's this?"

"Good, but I know you can do better."

Again he shortened the distance between them. "This close 'nough?"

"That'll do just fine. Now, I wonder if I can get you to do something else for me?"

"What?"

"Here," she said, reaching out, "I want you to put your hand in mine."

Snake tensed. "Look, Rev', I don't like getting touching-close to folks. That...that can leave you hurting. I tried that one Christmas years ago. Was a *bad* mistake."

"So you're afraid I'll harm you in some way?" Mary asked. Tentatively, as if approaching an open flame, he eased his hand forward. His and Mary's fingers touched. "What's wrong, son? Is it cold in here? You're...you're trembling."

"Me? Tremble? Naw, lady, I don't do that. That's a sign of weakness, and I ain't got no weaknesses. So tremble? No way, not *me!*"

"Guess I was mistaken." Mary gently caressed his Snake's hand. The trembling, *"non-trembling"* hand, gradually calmed.

"Yes, m'am, guess you was mistaken 'bout me trembling."

"Sorry."

"It's OK. Was a honest mistake."

"Glad you're so understanding, son."

Touching another human, a rarity for Snake Johnson, he felt a tide swell inside, flooding a drought he'd known nearly all his life. "Rev', I..."

"Son, don't I hear you crying?"

"'*Course not!*" After reconsidering, he sighed, "Yes, m'am, you heard right."

"Come down here closer to me. Then I want you to let it out, you understand? Let it all out."

"I can't."

The street hustler lowered to his knees and surrendered his face to the therapy of her touch. "You'll be alright, son," she soothed, massaging his face. "You'll be alright. I'm here for you. I'll always be here for you, son."

Several minutes later, after his emotions were spent, Mary said, "Robert, you'll find a box of tissues on that bureau over there. It might be a good idea if you got yourself a couple?"

"Yes, m'am."

He walked to the bureau and plucked several tissues from the box, then dabbed his cheeks. As he stood at the door, he said, "Rev'."

"Yes, Robert."

"Ah, want-cha to promise me something."

"What?"

"Promise me that you won't tell nobody what I did here."

"I don't follow."

"What I'm trying to say is, I wouldn't want word to get on the street that I, Snake Johnson, cried...ah, I mean...ah...had runny eyes."

"Oh, that. Trust me, my lips are sealed, son."

"Thanks. It's just that I'm 'shame of what I did."

"Ashamed of cry...I mean, having runny eyes? Shouldn't be ashamed of that, Robert, it's a common thing. Happens all the time, in the *best* of families."

"Do?"

"Yes. And, Robert, for what it's worth, I think you'd be a better man today if you'd had your...eye problem one Christmas years ago. I think you know what I mean."

"Yes, m'am, I think I do. Ah, by the way."

"Yes."

"Merry Christmas, Rev'."

"Thank you and the same to you, Robert." Mary paused. "You know, I was just thinking it's a shame your Merry Christmas was so late in coming."

"Yes, m'am, it is. But at least it came. And thank God, I was able to spend a part of it, not in jail as usual, but with my...*my mother.*"

"With your mother?" Snake eyed the old woman. Neither spoke, yet volumes were said. He opened the door. "Ah, Robert, did you forget the forty dollars I told you was on the counter?"

"No, m'am."

"Guess that means you took it, right?" Snake didn't answer. "Well, did you?"

"'Course I didn't! I'm *hurt* you'd even think I'd do a thing like that!"

"You don't have to shout, Robert. Besides, I was certain I knew the answer before I asked the question."

"Certain, you say?"

"Yes, son."

"How could you know if I took the money or not?"

"How?"

"Yes, m'am."

The blind woman paused, smiled, then said, "Good night, Robert."

"Ah, 'night, Rev'."

Snake stared at the preacher. He was amazed at how well she, an old sightless woman, could see, while his biological mother, with two good eyes, was totally blind.

✳ *Chapter Eleven*

Pain stabbed Louella's womb like a bowie knife. The agony persisted, seemingly determined to possess her, to become her body's sole tenant and torturer. Sometimes at night when the stabbing pain was worse, she imagined herself detaching from her body, hovering above the bed, then gazing down at a mass of misery. Though she had suffered this way off and on for weeks, she never told Willie.

Each evening, she watched him plod into their room, bone tired, back hurting. Thus, she considered it unthinkable to speak of *her* pain. Though bad, hers seemed a minor matter compared to the back pain he, in freezing coldness, silently endured every day. And so she suffered in solitude. However, instead of time erasing the hurt, it seemed to magnify it.

That night she and Willie lay in bed. He slept. She was awake, suffering through the stabbing pain. Clouds of thoughts floated before her. She sorted through them in an effort to review their problems:

Willie's bad back, his lack of a job, zero funds, no food, their possible eviction and the imminent birth of her baby.

Louella tried to fight off the depressing thoughts. Yet they loomed in front of her like menacing hungry monsters ready to devour everyone and everything in their path. In an effort to stave off her overwhelming fears, she tried to imagine what her child would look like. But doing so only reminded her that they had no crib or other essentials for the child. What would they do? How would they care for the offspring?

Thinking of her baby triggered the recall of an event long stored in a locker of her mind. When the incident took place, she gave it little thought. But now, looking at it through adult eyes, and remembering Blind Mary's prophesy, she was certain it had meaning. But what, she didn't know.

Slowly the incident loomed before her internal eye. She saw it as vividly as the day it happened.

At the time, her mother, Leatha, was pregnant. In the front yard of their shack, Louella, nearly ten, pendulumed back and forth on a tree swing. It was a pleasant sunny Piedmont afternoon. Wild blossoms carpeted the mountains. Cardinals chirped. Bees hummed as they flew among the honeysuckles that sweetened the already perfumed Virginia air.

Suddenly a woman screamed, her voice shattering tranquility. "Oh my *God*...oh my..." The alarm came from the shack where Louella's mother lay. "*Mercy, Jesus, mercy!* Lou', child, the pain, it's more than I can bear!"

Louella bolted towards the shack. "Momma, I'm coming!" When she reached the door, she rammed her shoulder into it; it flung open. Her mother, trembling, lay across the bed, her face a diagram of pain.

"Can't stand it no longer... Just can't stand it!"

"Momma, what's the matter?"

"Child, my baby, it's on its way!"

"Your baby? I don't know what to do!"

"Lou', scoot down the road yonder to the hollow and fetch Ole Lady Sadler. She's a midwife. Tell'er I'm 'bout to give birth. And tell'er to come *quick*."

"Momma, I--"

"Don't tarry, child, go!"

"Yessum."

Within minutes, Louella stood on the rickety porch of Miss Sadler's shack. With both fists, she pounded the door. "Bam...bam!"

"Who there? What-cha want?"

"Miss Sadler, Miss Sadler!"

"I hear-ya, child? No need to yell. Now what in tarnation is the matter?"

"Momma said you gotta come! Said the baby's 'bout to be born! Hurry, please *hurry*!"

"On my way! Gimme a second or so to gather my things."

When Louella and the midwife entered the patient's shack, Leatha was still lying across the bed. As if straining to bend them, she gripped the metal bedposts.

"Now, child, hear me good," Miss Sadler

instructed.

"Yessum."

"And don't tarry. Step yonder to that bureau and fetch a towel or a real clean rag. Go to the sink and get a bar of your momma's lye soap. Then pour some hot water in a wash basin. And oh yeah, look in the cabinet yonder and grab a butcher knife, sharpest your momma got!"

Louella scurried. When she'd gathered the requested items and placed them on the little table near the bed, she stood beside Miss Sadler, who now leaned over Leatha's spread legs.

"Child, maybe you'd betta step outside now," Miss Sadler said.

"I--"

"Ain't nothing else you can do in here."

"But, Miss Sadler, I'm afraid to leave."

"Go now, ya hea'?"

"Yes, m'am." Mesmerized by the tableau of pain, Louella continued standing.

"Well? Get out! Go!"

"Yes, m'am, I'm goin'." Louella's bare feet clawed the floor.

"Look, child, I *know* you heard me."

Finally the ten year old unriveted herself from the spot and ambled outside. Meanwhile, Leatha screamed again and again, each alarm more chilling. Then...eery silence. Shortly thereafter, a baby cried. Followed by more silence.

Minutes later, the door of the shack creaked open. Miss Sadler, haggard and drained, stepped onto the angled porch, squeaking the floorboards.

Blood stained her apron and her hands. "Child."

"Yes, m'am."

"Lord knows I did the best I could, the *very* best."

"How's momma? How's the baby?"

"Lou', it was just God's will. Their time had come. Their time had just come, child."

"My momma...I want my momma!"

"I understand child, of course you want her."

Louella cradled her face in her hands and sobbed as Miss Sadler hurried into the shack. When the midwife reappeared, she, with a towel, wiped blood from her hands. After draping the towel over her shoulder, she said, "Step over here to me, child." Louella hesitated but finally inched forward. Miss Sadler grasped the youngster's shoulders. "Louella."

"Yessum."

"You got reason 'nough for tears, no question 'bout that. But trust me, heaven called your kin 'cause it has something *special* planned for you, child. And that's the gospel truth. You see, after your momma and baby brother passed, I sensed a *strange* presence enter the room, and then I heard a voice. It said that you, Louella, are the chosen *one*, that through *your* womb a new Christmas will be born. One that will remind us of the real reason for Christmas. Your child will remind everyone of another child born so long ago."

"Miss. Sadler, I don't know what none-a that mean."

"The voice said you wouldn't, but that one day

you will, as will the world."

"Miss Sadler, I..." Louella's eyes flooded.

"It's alright, child, go 'head, wash away your sorrow with tears. Just remember what the voice said. Don't *never* forget it, that one day a new Christmas will come, and you have been chosen to give birth to it."

As Louella lay beside Willie, the midwife's words echoed in her thoughts. But if what the old woman said were true, she wondered why she, Louella Peterson, of all women, was "the selected one." She was a nobody -- a poor, uneducated, housewife. And because of her recurring pain, only a part-time housewife at that. So why...*her*?

She looked at the lone window in their room. Snow flurries speckled the night. Minutes later she closed her eyes. Then, suddenly jerked them open.

Seconds earlier she glimpsed a circular glow near the window. In its center, a face appeared. Vanished. Then reappeared. She rubbed her eyes.

As clearly as she now saw snowflakes, she had seen the face. Amber surrounded it like a corona edging an autumn moon. But now, no face, no glow. Nothing. Nothing but darkness.

In an instant, the face reappeared. Louella, heart pounding with fear, stared at the apparition. Its features seemed familiar. Could it be? Yes, it *was* the face of Miss Sadler. No sooner had she recognized it, then it was gone. Seconds later, however, it rematerialized.

"Louella," a voice said.

"Ah...yes...yes?"

"Step to the window."

"To the...window?"

"Hurry, child, my time is fleeting, hurry."

Being careful not to awaken Willie, Louella sat on the edge of the bed and slipped on her tattered bedroom slippers, then went to the window.

"Now, look at the street below." She did. "Tell me, what do you see?"

"The usual people, homeless men, panhandlers, hustlers, loiterers, runaways." Louella paused. "I don't understand. Miss Sadler, you're...you're dead. You died of consumption, years ago. Why have you returned?"

"To remind you of your mission, child."

"I haven't forgot. But, Miss Sadler, why am I the *'chosen one'*?"

"You answer your own question," the face smiled.

"How?"

"By raising the question, you show you are meek, and therefore worthy."

"But, Miss Sadler, I don't deserve no--"

"Saying you don't, is all more reason you do."

"I don't understand."

"That doesn't matter."

"Miss Sadler, what is the meaning of all of this?"

"Meaning? Child, all around you, Christmas dies. Through you, it will be reborn."

"Why's it dying?"

"You saw the answer."

"I did? When? Where?"

"Saw it when you looked out the window."

"What do you mean?"

"I ask again, what did you see?"

"Like I said, homeless men, panhandlers and hustlers."

"No, child, you saw more."

"I did?"

"Though you did not know it, you saw human deception, greed and coldness, and all of this, sadly, at Yuletide. What you didn't see was a single act of Christmas charity and love."

"I still don't understand."

"My stay must end shortly. The Great Spirit, I hear Him call my name."

"Are you ever coming back?"

"Yes."

"When?"

"When needed."

"When'll that be?"

"When greed again threatens man's only hope, the salvation of Yuletide love."

"Miss Sadler, can't you, can't you at least tell me--"

"Farewell, child. Farewell. I must depart now."

The dead woman's image vanished.

As she crawled back into bed Louella's first impulse was to awaken Willie and tell him of the visitor. She decided not to. How could she ask her husband, in fact, ask *anyone* to believe the face of a dead woman appeared, not only that, but spoke to her, and she to it?

Louella winced and closed her eyes. Several times she pried them open and gazed at the window, hoping Miss Sadler's face would be there. It wasn't. Meanwhile, the pain in her womb grew worse. She got up and took an aspirin. The pill didn't help. Her agony only intensified and, at times, sucked the breath out of her with its fanged jaws. She made a crucial decision. She would tell Willie of her suffering, tell him that she'd have to see a doctor. Whether they could afford it or not, she needed help. And soon.

✱ *Chapter Twelve*

Though she vowed she would, the following morning Louella couldn't bring herself to tell Willie of her pain. She tried. Hard. The words she planned to use formed in her thoughts, even journeyed to her lips. But once there, they balked. Out of compassion for him -- not wanting to add to his already-heavy burdens -- she couldn't tell him. Not that morning, that is. She'd let him know later, when he returned from work, but no, not that morning, not when the temperature outside was freezing and Willie had to face it.

At eight that night, Willie slid his key into the lock, opened the door, then stepped inside. Once there, he froze. He heard no movement, no hellos. Saw no smiles. Louella, silent, lay stretched across the bed, gazing at the ceiling, paying her husband no mind, as if he were invisible.

"Lou'."

"Yeah."

"Lou'...baby...what's wrong?"

"Ah, close the door, will-ya, Willie?" Quickly, he did. "Mind stepping over here?"

After moving to the bed, he stopped. "I hate having to say this, but you ain't looking too good, Lou'. And don't tell me you're OK, 'cause your eyes say otherwise."

"Naw, Willie, I won't tell-ya I'm OK, not no more." He sat on the edge of the bed and. "Willie, I want-cha to listen to me." He did, straining as Louella researched his eyes.

"I'm listening, Lou'."

"Willie, there's something I gotta tell-ya. For a long while now, I been shielding you from the truth; I just didn't feel I should add another cross to those you already carry."

"Shouldn't-a done that, Lou', 'cause whatever you locked inside yourself would-a been lighter to carry if we'd shouldered it together."

"Well, I understand that now," she responded quietly.

"Anyway, what is it you been holding from me?"

"To begin with, Willie, I don't have to tell-ya, though nine months pregnant, I ain't been to see no doctor, not once. We both know why. We ain't got no money or insurance. I never complained, but the truth is, lately I been having these sharp pains that 'bout to drive me crazy. Knowing we couldn't afford doctor care, I just suffered through the pain...*until now.*"

"Baby, want-cha to understand I feel *bad* that you couldn't see no doctor, real bad. But God as my witness, I been doing the *best* I can."

"Willie, I know how hard you try, I do. But, with this pain getting worser, we gone have to do something."

"Sure, Lou'."

"Willie, I just gotta see a doctor and soon!"

"I understand, but the question is, what'll we use for money, Lou'. Now-a-days, doctors charge a fortune, not to mention the cost of 'scriptions."

"I know."

"Why, just the other day, a woman was telling me 'bout a single 'scription for her rheumatism that cost ninety dollars, and that was just for three pills, too. That aside though, there has to be something we can do...somewhere we can go." He scratched his head. "What about...what about them free clinics?"

"What about'em?"

"There oughtta be at least one in this neighborhood...somewhere!"

"If there is, I sure don't know where."

"Me neither, but I figure it's just a matter of locating it. Some kinda' way."

"How we do that?"

"I don't know. Maybe I can find out from that storefront preacher 'round the corner. He's always helping folks. Every morning 'fore dawn I see lights on in his church. Tomorrow I'll stop by and ask'm."

"Would you, Willie?"

"'Course I will. I just can't have you suffering like this, Lou', I just can't."

"Willie, I want you to understand I wouldn't complain if the pain won't so bad."

"You don't have to apologize, Lou'."

She slid her hand into his as both turned and looked out the lone window. Diamonds of falling snow glistened in the darkness.

"That snow's sure pretty, ain't it, Willie? Remind me of Christmas back home in them Piedmont mountains."

"Yeah, it do. 'Course, back there, just like here, we was poor, but there it didn't seem we was, leastwise, not at Christmas."

"You're right. Christmas there sure ain't like it is here, is it? Here it's a rat race. Folks is shopping like crazy, fighting to buy what money can't really buy 'cause it ain't for sale. Wonder if folks will ever learn that, Willie?"

"Doubtful...very doubtful."

Two hours later, while they lay in bed, Willie began telling Louella how his day went. He told her of the apartment building on "H" Street that recently opened. Its new tenants, he said, discarded huge piles of packing crates which he picked up and sold, bringing in a few extra dollars.

On and on he monologued as she hung on every word. Opening up, unburdening themselves was something they routinely did at end of the day. Each always listened attentively because, as Louella put it, "everybody deserve a sympathetic ear."

Eventually, Willie realized Louella was no longer listening.

"Lou'."

"Yeah?"

"Are you--"

"Am I what?"

"Are you 'wake?"

"Yeah."

"Did you hear what I was telling you?"

"I heard, Willie."

"You sure?"

"Trust me, I heard. You sound kinda' surprised that I was paying attention to you."

"Well, you was so...you know, quiet, like your mind was in another place."

"Sorry. But, if you wanna know the whole truth, while you was conversating, my mind did wander a little. I started thinking 'bout something you mentioned a while back."

"What?"

"Do you remember that old blind preacher you spoke of and what she said?"

"'Course I remember her. She said you'd have a special child that would change Christmas back to what it should be, what it should mean in people's hearts."

"Talk like that, sure make a body pause, don't it?"

"Yeah, it do."

"I was laying here asking myself if there's any truth to what she said."

"Only God knows, Lou'."

"That's for sure. But, Willie, if the preacher's right, I can't help but think 'bout the future of my child. Considering all that's going on today -- you know, drive-by shootings, muggings, drugs -- a mother can't help but wonder how her child will survive in today's wicked world. Is he or she likely to live long 'nough to even become a teenager, let alone a man or a woman? Especially in this neighborhood."

"Lou', now don't you fret none, you hear? I'm sure our kid'll be OK and make it just like all the other teens 'round here."

"Make it? And what will that mean, Willie? Will it mean you and me will be worried sick all the time, fearful our child'll be gunned down in a alley somewhere or shot in a drive-by? Then, like others murdered, be forgotten, just another name on a piece of paper, another body in a bag? Or while walking to school, like so many today, he or she'll be robbed of tennis shoes or jacket. And if our child don't give'm up fast 'nough, somebody'll put a bullet through its brain. Then too, there's the chance he'll end up a drug pusher and drive one-a them fancy limos bought with others' blood and broken lives."

"Gotta admit, Lou', everything you say could happen."

"Or worse, Willie."

"But, trust me, Lou', it won't. See, you're forgettin' one thing."

"What?"

"If our child is gonna be *special* like the preacher say, special enough to change Christmas and all, if he's that special, I expect he'll be able to overcome a few...tribulations. Even be strong enough to survive living near that crack house at Fourteenth and U, you know, the one folks talk 'bout all the time. So, Lou', don't worry none, you hear?"

"Hope you right."

"I know I am."

"Willie."

"Yeah?"

"Funny you should mention that house at Fourteenth and U. Just the other day Mrs. Lewis who live down the hall was talking 'bout it. She said even the police is nervous 'bout going in that place. Said that disturbances is so common there, folks who hear screams coming from inside, just hurry on by and don't pay it no mind."

"That don't surprise me none." For a few minutes, neither spoke. Finally Willie said, "Lou'."

"Huh?"

"I thought you'd dozed off."

"No, I'm still 'wake."

"Ah, maybe you'd better try to get some rest, 'cause if I find a clinic for you tomorrow, you'll have to walk to it, and we don't know how far that'll be. So you'd better get some sleep. OK?"

"Sure, Willie."

Soon Louella dozed.

He snuggled closer to her. Gazing into the dark silence, he wondered if his wife, as the preacher predicted, would in fact have a "special child." One like no earthly child ever born, capable of doing things never done before. A child who would touch lives, inspiring people to honor that *special baby* born so long ago, the true reason for Christmas.

✳ *Chapter Thirteen*

Early the following morning Willie and Louella lay in bed, she, asleep, he, gazing at the ceiling.

"Tick...tock...tick...tock..." The old dented wind-up clock, salvaged from a trash can, dialogued with itself. "Tick...tock...tick...tock." He carefully reached over his wife and switched the alarm off, then lay back down. As he did, the bed springs squeaked. The sound awakened Louella.

"You getting up now?" she yawned.

"Yeah. Didn't mean to wake-ya."

"That's OK. Won't sleeping too good no ways."

"'Bout the way I slept, too. You feeling any pain now?"

"No," she lied. "Ah, the alarm, did it ring?" she asked, hoping to change the subject.

"Naw, I switched it off. I thought I'd make a early start to see if I can find a clinic."

"Sure hope you can."

"If I find one, I'll come back for you, Lou'."

"OK. Ah, lemme get up and fix you a piece of toast for breakfast."

"Doing that might cause your pain to come back. I'll do it, baby. No botha."

After breakfast, Willie touched a kiss to Louella's cheek, walked to the door and stopped.

"Lou'."

"Yeah."

"Gotta tell-ya, I feel bad 'bout somethin'."

"What?"

"Well, with so *much* weighting my thoughts lately -- overdue rent, the fact we broke, the pain you're in, the -- "

"And your own back problem, Willie. You didn't mention that."

"Well, that ain't nothing, Lou', but if you insist I'll add it. Anyway, with so many things crowding my thoughts, I'm 'shame to admit it, but I completely forgot to wish you a Merry Christmas. So, Merry Christmas, Lou'."

"Thanks, and the same to you."

"Lou', I sure hope next Christmas will be betta to us than this one has been."

"It will. You gotta remember, Willie, life don't come with no guarantees."

"That's for sure. Anyway, 'bye, Lou'."

"'Bye, Willie."

He headed down the stairs, being careful to walk to the left, for directly overhead a huge hole gaped in the ceiling. Plaster, he feared, might fall at any moment, as it had two weeks earlier. Like other tenants, he had learned that walking the hall stairs could be hazardous. Gusts nipped as he closed the vestibule door and leaned into morning coldness. He had walked a half a block when he stopped beside The Capital Diner and looked inside. Behind the counter, the owner, Leon, poured hot coffee into a customer's mug. Beside the mug sat a plate heaped with linked sausages, scrambled eggs, pancakes and fried potatoes, all generating little clouds of steam. Willie gazed at the tempting meal and remembered the two slices of dry toast he'd had for breakfast. Sighing, he pressed his collar to his neck and continued down Florida Avenue.

A woman in her late twenties, a short black skirt hugging her thighs like rubber gloves, stood shivering near the corner, occasionally breathing warmth across her fingers.

"Hey, sport!" she chirped, hailing Willie.

"Yeah."

"You in the market for a little...*action*?"

"Lady, I got more pressing things on my mind this morning: like getting my wife to a free clinic."

"What's wrong with'er?"

"Pregnant and sick as a dog."

"When she expecting?"

"Any day now."

"Oh."

"You wouldn't happen to know where there's a free clinic 'round here, would-cha?"

"Can't help-ya there. See, I don't live in DC. Just here temporary."

"Where-ya from?"

"Baltimore."

"Long way from home, ain't-cha?"

"Ain't that far: just a couple dollars and change by Greyhound. Anyway, Baltimore sure ain't no place for a working girl at Christmas time -- business drags. Me? I need money now, *bad*. See, I promised my little girl Santa would bring her one-a them talking Serena dolls for Christmas. 'Course, I made the same promise last year. I couldn't keep it though. How could I, flipp'n' 'burgers at Wendy's for minimum?"

"There ain't no way you can get rich doing that."

"Mista, know what it's like to listen to your kid bawl her eyes out on Christmas morning 'cause Santa didn't come? Ain't easy. I learned that last year. And to make matters worse, this year, department stores *tripled* the price on them dolls -- the crooks." Her eyes brightened. "Know what'd be nice?"

"Naw, what?"

"Be nice if at Christmas, instead-a making merchants richer, folks gave each other gifts of love and warmth. Neither cost nothing and even Lord and Taylor can't match'em."

"That's for sure."

"But of course I'm talking about giving real love, not the kind I sell."

"Think folks'll ever take your advice?"

"Maybe. Who knows? Meanwhile, I gotta make some money for my kid's doll. So, guess I'll have to go on peddling the only love that sells in this neighborhood. Anyway, like I said, about that free clinic...wish I could help-ya." She paused. "Wait. Just thought, you might stop by that storefront church 'round the corner and ask the Reverend there. Maybe he can help."

"I'd planned to go there. Do you know the preacher?"

"Well, I've met him. Yesterday he stopped me and gave me a sidewalk sermon and a prayer. He prayed God would guide me from 'the sinful ways of the flesh.'"

"Think God will?"

"If he do, hope he'll wait till after Christmas. 'Cause I need that doll money *now*. As for that Reverend Myers, I'd like him to be the one to dry my daughter's eyes when she find out Santa was a no-show again."

Two men in hardhats and carrying lunch pails approached. The prostitute winked at them. "Ah, excuse me," she said to Willie. "I gotta get back to work."

"Sure, I understand."

She stepped to the left, blocking the two pedestrians. "Hey, sports, look like you guys could use a little companionship, a little love." The three chatted, negotiating a price. After agreeing on one, they left.

Willie watched the "love" merchant and her patrons enter a nearby flop house. He shivered. The temperature was now near freezing. Flipping up his collar and bristling, Willie continued walking.

✽ *Chapter Four*

The following morning Blind Reverend Mary, white cane in hand, groped east along Seventh Street."

"Tap...tap...tap..."

Using her cane, she tattooed the curb, making sure she hadn't strayed too close to the street. A misstep could result in injury, a fact she knew well, for the previous year she had tripped and toppled into the path of a swerving Yellow Cab. The result was a fractured ankle and a month's convalescence in DC General Hospital.

"Tap...tap...tap..."

Mary hated hospitals, in fact, she hated all things confining. In spite of her blindness, she enjoyed being unfettered, active: she relished rising early, walking to her "church," preaching, conversing with friends, visiting the sick, going here and there. She was an independent, liberated spirit. She never had to remind herself of this -- others, yes, and often, especially those who saw her as helpless.

"Tap...tap...tap..."

Now at the bus stop. she heard footsteps to her rear.

"Morn', Rev'."

"Morning, 'Shorty.'"

Shorty's legal name was Stratton Louis Allepo. Along Florida Avenue, however, everyone knew him as "Shorty." The middle-aged mail clerk was once a lush. For months, off and on, Mary counseled him, hoping to help her friend conquer his drinking problem. During his many relapses, three or more a month, she braced him with patience and understanding, encouraging him to have faith in his potential. Finally, he did. And thanks to Mary, he hadn't touched the bottle in over a year.

"How-ya like this weather, Shorty?"

"Too windy for me."

"Same here."

"I'm all for a white Christmas, yes, but freezing winds I can do without."

"Shorty, like you, most people adore white Christmases; they retrieve memories of old friends and good times."

"No doubt 'bout that. By the way, Mary, kinda odd seeing you this far down on Seventh Street."

"Had to come here to transfer to the Number Seven bus."

"Where-ya headed?"

"Upper New Hampshire Avenue. I've got some important business there, Shorty. It's urgent I talk to Bishop Richfield."

"Bishop Richfield?"

"Yes."

"You don't mean *The* Bishop Donald Richfield, do you, pastor of that church in the ritzy section of New Hampshire Avenue?"

"The same."

"Well, never figured you and The Bishop would have all that much in common, Mary. I mean, he's, you know, upper crust and all."

"So I'm told."

"Think you'll feel comfortable in that, ah, *silk stocking* neighborhood?"

"I'm sure I will, thanks to the blessing God gave me."

"Blessing?"

"Yes. Blindness, Shorty. Blindness. You see, to the blind, all neighborhoods are the same. Anyway, as I said, today I have crucial news I must share with The Bishop."

"You make it sound like it's a matter of life and death, Mary."

"It is, Shorty -- the most *important* news ever heard."

"You mean, heard by The Bishop, don't-cha?"

"No, Shorty...heard by *the world*."

"Well now, if I ain't being too nosey, Mary, what is this important news?"

"Be happy to tell you. You see--"

"Scre-e-e-e-ch..." At the icy curb a Metro Transit Authority bus jerked to a stop.

"It's your bus, Mary -- Number Seven."

"At last."

"Before you go, wanna thank you for my

Christmas gift."

"Christmas gift, Shorty?"

"Yeah, I mean, the way you helped me sober up. Without you, Mary, I'd probably be laying in some gutter right now, stoned, instead of sober and looking forward to Christmas...with hope."

"The credit belongs to you, Shorty, not me."

"Mary, your modesty is as big as your heart."

Shorty helped his friend board the bus, then guided her to a seat near the entrance. "Driver, mind letting Reverend Mary off at the home of Bishop Richfield?"

"Home?" the bus driver chuckled. "You mean, castle, don't-cha?"

"You're right there. A castle *is* more like it. Anyway, do ya' mind?"

"Happy to."

Twenty minutes later the driver announced, "This here's your stop, Rev'. Ah, you need help?"

"No, thanks, I believe I can manage."

"Sure?"

"Quite."

Mary felt her way to the exit. Seeing a passing postman, the driver hailed him and asked if he'd escort the evangelist to Bishop Richfield's residence. He agreed.

Standing before the portal of the palatial home, Mary raised the ornate brass knocker with her gloved hand. "Bam...Bam...Bam!" Soon, the door opened and a middle-aged woman, face chiseled from granite, appeared. Her maid's uniform was spotless, impeccably pressed.

sidewalks. Willie approached Clipper Jones Tourist Home. The front door of the flop house opened and a woman appeared.

"Hey!" she called out to Willie. It was the streetwalker whose daughter wanted Santa to bring a Serena Doll.

"Hey yourself! How-ya doing?"

"*Now* I'm doing just *fine*. Just fine! Guess what? Santa's gonna bring my baby her doll, thank God."

"Happy for you both."

"Thanks."

"Well," Willie said, "take care of yourself. Stay safe, you hear'?"

"I will."

"And your daughter, do the same for her."

"Taking care of her, that go without saying."

"I just know she'll love that doll Santa'll bring her."

"Yeah. Seeing it, her beautiful eyes'll light up like stars." The streetwalker paused. "Hey, know something? Just had an idea. Wouldn't it be nice if I wrote a little note and pinned it to the doll?"

"What'd it say?"

"Oh, I don't know, something like...ah...thanks to you, I can feel Christmas again. I'd forgotten how."

"Sound good."

"Yeah, it does. Thanks. Well, nice talking to-ya. Guess I'd betta head to the bus station."

"Ya goin' back to Baltimore?"

"Yeah."

The two hardhats the prostitute had serviced exited the tourist home. Seeing her, they turned and walked in the opposite direction.

"Ah, have a merry Christmas," she said to Willie.

"Now that your daughter'll get her doll, I'm sure *yours* will be the merriest."

"Yes, the merriest."

That was the last time Willie saw the woman. He never forgot her, though. Or the doll Santa Claus brought her daughter that Christmas morning.

✳ *Chapter Fifteen*

When Willie returned to his room, Louella, almost asleep, lay across the bed.

"That you, Willie?"

"Yeah. How-ya feeling?"

"'Bout the same," she said, hiding her pain.

"Were you able to find out 'bout the clinic?"

"Yeah. Preacher at that little storefront gave me the address. Said it should be opening 'bout now. So you better start putting on your things, Lou'."

"OK. Ah, how far 'way is it?"

"Ain't far. Shouldn't take us long."

Willie was right. Fifteen minutes later, they stood in front of The Northwest Community Free Health Center. Starting at its entrance, a line backed up for a quarter of a block.

"Heavens!" Louella gasped, hand covering her swollen abdomen, "look...at...that line! Will ya just look at..."

"I'm looking, Lou', I'm looking."

"Ever seen anything like it, Willie? Who'd

dream there'd be so many folks here and so early, too."

"So many poor folks, you mean, Lou'. Rich folks don't stand in lines. Guess the preacher was right."

"'Bout what?"

"He warned we'd have a long wait. I figured there'd be a line, but nothing like this."

"Think we'll *ever* get in there, Willie?"

"Sure. But the trick is gone be getting out...any time today, that is."

"Or ever."

They walked to the end of the line. Fifteen minutes later, the door of the clinic opened and an employee with a bullhorn pressed to his lips stepped to the sidewalk. "Listen up, people. Now I don't want anybody stampeding, you heah? In due time you'll all get to see the doctor. It's just gonna take patience, patience. Understand?"

Little by little, the line inched forward. Finally inside, Willie and Louella found two empty chairs near the rear of the waiting room and sat.

Three hours later, they were still sitting. To help pass the time, Willie squirmed, fidgeted, crossed his legs, uncrossed them, over and over. He was anxious to do something, *anything* to enable his wife to see the doctor faster. But what? How could he clear the room of those ahead of Louella? Or, that failing, somehow place her at the front of the line? He, of course, knew the answer to both questions. He couldn't. And impossible.

Louella, in spite of her pain and the endless

wait, wasn't as anxious as Willie. She uttered no complaints and contented herself by flipping through one magazine after another, or, tiring of that, studying the faces of those sitting near her. From their expressions, she tried to fathom what misfortune visited them this Christmas, as it had Willie and her, directing their lives to intersect in a waiting room, a holding place for those sharing a common problem -- poverty.

"Willie."

"Huh?"

"I been counting folks as they go in to see the doctor and I bet you can't guess how many've gone in so far?"

"Naw, I can't."

"In four hours, six."

"At that rate, God only know how long it'll take before the doc'll see you, Lou'."

"Bet not even God, in all his infinite wisdom, can be sure, Willie."

They laughed, but only briefly.

Later, Willie looked at the wall clock behind the receptionist's desk -- four-thirty. His legs and arms felt like cement-filled stumps. But worse, hunger now knotted his stomach. Louella, he reasoned, was probably as hungry as he, maybe hungrier.

"Lou', know you ain't complained none, but you gotta be starved."

"Well, the truth is, I am, but I know we don't have no money, so I didn't say noth'n'."

"Surprise, Lou', we do have some. It ain't much, though. Rummaging through a trash bin yesterday, I ran across a envelope with a little change in it -- dollar and sixty cents. So why don't I step 'round the corner to McDonald's and get you somethin'?"

"What 'bout yourself?"

"Don't worry 'bout me, I'll be alright."

"Willie, you gotta start thinking 'bout your *own* health and strength, not just mine."

"Face it, Lou', ain't no way we both can eat off a buck sixty."

"Guess-ya right."

"So, it's settled. The food'll be for you." He placed his hand on her belly. "You and the house guest," he smiled.

Outside, darkness now blanketed the city. Willie moved down the sidewalk into assaults of stinging gusts. The busy intersection was about fifty yards ahead, but because of freezing winds, the distance seemed longer. Finally he reached the corner, turned left, and a half block later, entered the McDonald's.

The eatery was almost empty. Three customers, all teenagers, two females, one male, sat in a booth near the entrance, not far from where Willie stood rubbing feeling back into his fingers. A Quarter Pounder sat on the table in front of each diner.

Willie stared at the food and imagined one of the sandwiches topping his palate, then sliding into his stomach.

"What's wrong, Keisha?" one teen said.

"Big problem, Yolanda."

"You mean--"

"Right. You got a, ah, you know what."

"Sure ain't."

"I gotta get one -- fast. Come on, girl, go with me."

"Sure."

The pair popped to their feet and scurried towards the door, leaving their Quarter Pounders and male friend behind.

"Hey!" the boy blurted, scooping up his sandwich. "Wait up!" The trio exited.

Willie wondered if the females would return for their food. He waited -- for about thirty seconds -- enough time to convince him they wouldn't. After wrapping the sandwiches in napkins, he picked up the orphaned meals and walked to the counter.

"What's yours?"

"What can I get for a buck sixty?"

"Single burger, small fries."

"Tax included?"

"Yep."

"Gimme that."

"Anything to drink?"

"Sure, if it's free."

Smileless, the bored clerk eyed Willie. "Here or to go?"

"Go."

"One burger and fries, coming up."

While he waited, Willie gobbled down the two Quarter Pounders. His empty stomach growling a welcome to the much needed food. "Oh, and, put some napkins with that, will-ya?"

Willie picked up his order and stepped outside into the night air. In the next block he noticed a group of men, all in their early twenties, who congregated on the sidewalk. One held a briefcase. Backpacks draped the shoulders of the others. Jabbering excitedly, they all pointed at the sky. Willie approached the man with the briefcase.

"What's going on? What's everybody staring at?"

"A comet."

"Where? I don't see nothin'."

"There, to the left."

"Oh. Now I see. Ah, what did you call that thing?"

"A comet."

"Look like a ordinary shooting star to me, the kinda thing you see all the time in summer."

"Trust me, mister, it's not, as you put it, just another 'ordinary shooting star.'"

"Ain't?"

"No."

"Well, I'm certainly learning something tonight. Me, I always called them things shoo... Anyway, a comet, you say is the right name?"

"Yeah, but that comet is not the run-of-the-mill kind. It's like no other ever seen."

"What make it different?"

"The tail, it's pointed in the wrong direction."

"What-cha mean?"

"See? The tail's aimed towards the sun."

"And that's the *wrong* way?"

"Sure is. That comet is turning the laws of

nature upside down. Doing things it shouldn't."

"Ain't natural, uh?" Willie said.

"Most...*unnatural*."

"Ah, tell me somethin'."

"What?"

"How come you know so much about shooting sta... I mean, whatever you call them things."

"Comets."

"Right, comets. How come you know so much 'bout'em?"

"I'm a grad student, so are the rest of these guys here. I've been studying the heavens for years. Hope to finish my dissertation next month."

"Your *what*?"

"Dissertation. Ah, that's a kind of book you have to write before they'll graduate you."

"Oh."

"Anyway, I've studied comets for quite a while, poring over charts and eyewitness accounts that go back before the time of Jesus Christ, even beyond the pyramids. And trust me, there's never been a comet like this one tonight, never." The scholar scratched his head. "Something odd is going on in the heavens, most *odd*. Years from now, I'm sure men will probably still be trying to understand it."

"You think so?"

"No doubt in my mind."

Eying the streaking phenomenon, Willie said, "Well, really do 'preciate what you taught me."

"No problem. I enjoyed the conversation. Comets, the moon, stars -- these things are my life." The student paused. "Know something?"

"What?"

"We're lucky. One day we'll be able to tell our children and grandchildren we witnessed this...this one-of-a-kind thing. Ah, you got any children?"

"No, but my wife's pregnant, probably deliver any day now -- boy I hope."

"Boy, uh?"

"Yeah, always wanted one."

"Same here. Well, hope your wife'll have a boy for you, and then you'll be able to tell your son about this amazing sight."

Willie, voice filled with awe, asked. "Wonder what it...wonder what it *all* mean?"

"Mean?"

"Yeah."

"Afraid I don't follow you."

"What I'm trying to say is that in olden days, folks claimed things like shooting stars...or...comets had a meaning, that they was a sign of what's to come."

"Well, I'm a student of astronomy. I study heavenly bodies, what they're made of, why they exist, how long they'll live, and the like. As for what comets mean, well, for that you'll have to talk to somebody else, a prophet, or divine messenger maybe. You wouldn't happen to know one, would you?" the grad student smiled.

"Yes."

"Oh? Well, you'd better ask him. Perhaps he'll be able to answer your question."

"It's a *she*, and I'm beginning to think she's already answered it."

"Oh? What'd she say?"

"Ah, nothing."

"Nothing? I don't get your meaning."

"What I mean is, she said nothing that'd make sense to folks trained to understand numbers and charts, but who can see nothing beyond."

"Oh," the astronomy student said, "...I see."

✳ *Chapter Sixteen*

"See you made it back OK," Louella said as Willie eased into the chair beside her.

"Yeah, did."

"Still cold out?"

"That wind is slicing like a straight razor." He handed her the bag of food.

"Thank-ya, Willie."

Louella lost little time in eating the sandwich. As she raised the last fry to her lips, Willie told her of the unique comet he saw. In mid air, she stopped the fry, lowered it, then searched his eyes. "Willie, you... don't suppose..."

"Suppose what?"

"You don't suppose that comet, it mean that our baby he--"

"Mrs. Louella Peterson!" the receptionist paged. "Mrs. Louella...Peterson!"

"Here!"

"You're next."

"Thank-ya, m'am. Be right there." Louella

faced her husband. "Come on, Willie, want-cha to go in with me."

"Go in with you?"

"'Course."

"Why? Ain't nothing I can do."

"I need you *beside* me, need your presence."

"Well, if you put it that way, 'course I'll go. But is it...is it gonna be alright for me to be in there with you?"

"I seen other couples go in together. One while you was at McDonald's."

"Oh."

"Mrs. Louella Peterson!" the receptionist repeated.

"Coming."

Willie and Louella entered the door leading from the waiting room into a long hall past several offices, all containing assortments of medical equipment. Neither of course knew for what purposes the devices were used, only that they looked, as Louella later put it, "sciencey."

Doctor Edwards' office was at the end of the corridor. Once in it, they noticed how sparsely the room was furnished: an old examination table, a glass-doored metal cabinet and a small desk; fronting the desk were two worn chairs. Willie and Louella sat in them.

Minutes later, Doctor Edwards lumbered in, his fatigue evident.

"Well, 'evening, all."

"'Evening," Louella said.

"Evening, doc'," Willie said, shifting

uncomfortably.

The graying physician eased into the chair behind his desk. As Louella described her many symptoms, his eyes riveted on her. Leaning forward, he sponged her every word, occasionally jotting notes or interrupting with a question.

When she finished, the physician massaged his chin. "Um-m. Well-l-l-l-l, Mrs. Peterson," he sighed, "there are several possible explanations for the discomfort you describe. But the most likely cause is that your baby has assumed an unnatural position in the womb. That often happens. And when it does, the result is discomfort similar to that you experience. For me to determine if this is the cause, we'll have to perform the necessary test...or tests."

"This, ah, test, is it gonna be hard, doc'?" Louella asked nervously.

"No, quite simple."

"But will it hurt?"

"Not in the least."

"Sure happy to hear *that*," she sighed in relief.

"In one of the nearby rooms I have equipment that'll take a kind of -- um-m-m, how can I put this? -- a kind of, ah, motion picture of your child and its position in the uterus, I mean, womb."

"Can you really do that?"

"Easily."

"And it ain't gonna hurt none, you say?"

The doctor's smile mirrored his fatherly patience. "Why, you'll scarcely feel a thing, Mrs. Peterson."

"Good," she sighed. By the way, is it alright if

my husband come in with me?"

"No problem."

"Now, doc'," Willie hesitated, his nervousness showing, "wouldn't wanna get in your way none."

"You won't. So if you two'll just follow me, we'll get started."

"Yes, sir."

The physician led the couple down the hall and into a room containing an examination table. On a stand beside it sat a rectangular device, on top of this, a monitor, the two coupled by cables.

"Now, Mrs. Peterson, disrobe down to your waist, please, then lie on the table. This whole exam shouldn't take long. And do relax. As I said, you'll experience no discomfort."

"Yes, sir."

After taking off her clothing, Louella sat on the edge of the table. With Willie's help, she lay on her back.

"Are you comfortable, Mrs. Peterson?"

"Yes, sir."

"Excellent...excellent."

"When I say 'comfortable,'" the patient half smiled, "I mean, as comfortable as someone lugging a watermelon in her belly can be."

"I'm sure pregnancy can't be a fun thing," the doctor chuckled. "And you'd think the man, the stronger, would be the one to carry the watermelon, wouldn't you?"

"Sure would."

"But," the doctor sighed, "nature knows her business, been doing it for millions of years. So who am I to..."

Doctor Edwards stepped to the machine. Lining its front panel were tiers of dials, toggle switches and buttons of various sizes, shapes, colors. He flipped one of the green switches. "Snap!" A little light above it glowed red. Slowly he turned a knob, all the while eying the meter to its left whose pointer fluttered, slowed and finally stopped. After applying a jelly-like substance to Louella's belly, he picked up a wand and gently placed it over her navel.

"See," he reassured, "doesn't hurt, does it?"

"Naw, sir. Not a bit."

The examiner peered at the monitor. Though lit, the screen remained blank. The wand he then inched up and down, right and left, all the while observing the monitor. It continued to show a blank. "Um-m-m-m...that *is* odd."

"What, doc'?"

"Oh, probably nothing, Mrs. Peterson. Just that I'm not getting a picture. Hold on a second, I want to check the oscillator." He flipped two of the switches on the lower tier of five, then pushed a little button. The meter's needle quivered, stopped, coming to rest on the number nine. "Well, seems the oscillator checks out OK. Um, let's try the device again, see what we get." He reapplied the probe to Louella's belly, then gazed at the monitor. Once again, a brightly lit, but image-free screen glowed. "Wel-l-l-l..."

"Still ain't having no luck, doc'?" Louella asked.

"None."

"What was you suppose to see?"

"Something like a negative of your baby, but with pictures that move, ah, sorta like a little movie. And by examining it, I can determine the fetus...I mean, your baby's position."

"Oh."

"Ah, Mrs. Peterson, mind excusing me for a second? I need step to my office and pick up the technical manual for this device. I think I can solve the problem."

"Hope-ya right."

Doctor Edwards left and soon returned with the manual. He buried his eyes in the large book. Now at the rear of the testing apparatus, he mumbled to himself, "Let me see now. The A-7 connection seems to be in place." He glanced first at the manual, then the cables attached to the machine's rear panel. "And the same is true for the A-9 connection. That leaves only the oscillator amplifier triodes. Are they coupled to the power circuitry? That is the question." He jiggled one connector, then another. "Well, they all appear to be OK. So everything seems in place. Suppose we try this again, Mrs. Peterson."

"Anything you say, doc'."

The physician flipped a switch and reapplied the wand. After studying the blank monitor, he frowned. Mystified, he scratched his head. "Now if this doesn't beat all," he mumbled.

"Still ain't getting nothin', doc'?"

"Not a thing, a perfect zero. I frankly don't

understand it. I mean, I've checked this device thoroughly -- all stages.

"Everything here indicates it's functioning properly. Besides that, it has a built-in diagnostic mechanism. That means it can show when there is something wrong, not only that, but what the problem is. And it reports *all* is working perfectly. Yet, when I apply the transducer -- ah, the wand -- no image of your child appears.

"Mrs. Peterson, I've worked with these machines for years and I've never had this happen. One doesn't have to be a medical genius to realize you're pregnant. You know that, I too; anyone with eyes should. Yet, the instrument shows no evidence that a baby exists in you. Instead, it reports it sees nothing. At least," the doctor mused, "sees nothing it can record. Whole thing's baffling. It's as if your baby, as far as the machine is concerned, has no *physical* body, is made of something other than the flesh and blood we're all made of. I'm...I'm...lost!"

"Hope that don't mean you can't give me nothing for my pain."

"Not at all, Mrs. Peterson."

"'Cause, sometimes, doc', the hurt, it just rip through me like barb wire."

"I can imagine, Mrs. Peterson. But as I say, I'll be able to help. I'll prescribe a rather potent multi...I mean, a strong many purpose pain killer." The physician stared at the monitor, as if drawn into its blankness. Minutes passed.

"Doc'."

"Huh, oh...ah, sorry, Mrs. Peterson, forgive me.

I'm afraid my thoughts wandered. Anyway, as I was saying, I'll prescribe something to relieve your discomfort."

"That's good. But, tell me, doc', I know this is a free clinic and all, but this special machine here, is you gonna have to charge me for being examined on it? 'Cause, my husband Willie and me, we ain't got no money."

"Won't cost you a dime."

"And I got the same question 'bout the 'scription you'll probably write for me, is we gonna have to pay for--"

"Absolutely not. I get free samples from drug companies all the time, and before you leave I'll give you a supply, enough to last a good while."

"'Preciate it."

"Yes, sir," Willie added, "we *sure* do."

"My pleasure."

The three returned to the doctor's office. "Excuse me a second: I have to step across the hall where I keep the medications locked up. Be right back." The physician exited.

"Willie," Louella whispered as soon as the door closed.

"Huh."

"The doctor, he ain't the *only* one confused by what's going on 'round here. I mean, why didn't he see a picture of my baby?"

"Maybe the trouble was in his machine after all."

"You heard'm, he said it was working just fine."

"Still, Lou', there's always the chance he made some kinda mistake."

"But he told us the machine could test itself. And the tester showed there won't *nothing* wrong with it. Yet, my baby didn't show up in the picture. Um, odd, real odd, ain't it?"

"Yeah, Lou', sure is."

When Doctor Edwards returned, he carried a small plastic bag. "Now, Mrs. Peterson," he said, removing several little foil packets from it, "here's the medication samples I mentioned. The labels indicate you should take one pill twice daily, with or without food, doesn't matter." After returning the foil packets to the bag, he handed the bag to Louella.

"Thank you, doc'."

The kind physician walked the patient and her husband to the door. "Well, Mrs. Peterson, after taking the medication, I'm sure you will feel much better -- and soon."

"Hope you right, doc'."

"I'm just sorry I couldn't do more. But as you saw, for reasons I don't understand, that machine of mine wouldn't give a readout -- ah, I mean, a picture -- of your baby."

"Ain't your fault, doc'."

"I always enjoy watching future mothers as they see images of the life they're about to deliver. But in your case, sadly, I'm afraid you won't have that pleasure." Doctor Edwards scratched his head and frowned. "Strange...strange," he muttered. "The medical journals will certainly delight in this one. They'll have a field day."

"Pardon, what was that, doc'?"

"Ah, nothing, Mrs. Peterson. That is, nothing that'd interest you. It was just...doctor talk."

"Oh. Anyway, thanks," Louella said.

"Yeah, you really helped me and my wife a lot." Willie shook the doctor's hand.

"Helping, that's what good medicine is all about."

"Pity all doctors don't think that way," Willie said as he helped Louella with her coat.

"You're very kind. Anyway, have a pleasant evening and a merry Christmas to you both."

"Same to you," the prospective parents said in unison.

Willie and Louella headed down the hall. After a few paces, they glanced back. Brow furrowed, Doctor Edwards stared deeply, probingly into space. "Unprecedented," he mumbled softly as he shook his head. "*Unprecedented!*"

Willie and Louella didn't know what "unprecedented" meant. They both thought it was just more "doctor talk," some fancy word which had no connection to them or their baby, who, as far as the doctor -- at least, his machine -- could determine, was as intangible as air or invisible as a spirit.

❋ *Chapter Seventeen*

The couple headed up New Jersey Avenue. Soon they neared the place where Willie chatted with the university student. Unlike earlier, the sidewalk there now teemed with people: men, women, young, old, the overflow spilling into the street, blocking traffic. All gazed at the comet, now brighter than when Willie saw it and seeming to move more slowly. In spite of freezing temperature, apartment tenants leaned out of windows and gazed at the sky.

"Willie," Louella gasped, "what in...what in the world's going on?"

"It's the comet, Lou'. Like I told-ya, folks are looking at it. Remember, I told you they--"

"I remember, but I thought you meant a *handful* of people, not no crowd this size."

"Was just a handful earlier."

"Sure ain't that now. 'Bout how many folks you figure out here?"

"Can't even start to guess, Lou'."

The throng seemed countless. Cars were locked in place, jammed bumper to bumper. Buses, unable to move, were parked, their seats empty. Bus passengers were on sidewalks and in the street, mesmerized by the celestial light show.

Oddly, in spite of the traffic gridlock, no motorist honked his horn, shouted obscenities, unprecedented in DC tie-ups, a city known for fender-benders, followed by squabbles, fist fights, sometimes gun fire.

Hoping to unsnarl the tangle, a cop at the intersection motioned cars forward. None moved. None could. The policeman shrugged, flung up his arms, stomped to the sidewalk, and, like others, gazed at the sky.

"Willie."

"Yeah."

"Ah...I...I hate to bring this up, but the pain, it's coming back."

"Bad?"

"Not real bad, not yet no ways, but it's getting worser. I'd betta get home and take my medicine."

"'Course, Lou'." A human wall blocked them. "'Scuse us," Willie said. "Ah, my wife, she's pregnant, *real* sick, gotta get'er home. Pardon us, please...par...." The mass before them stood impenetrable and immovable.

"Make way!" a voice exploded.

"Y'all heard the man!" someone added. "Lady's pregnant, let'er through."

Gradually a path parted before Willie and his

wife and they moved through it. At the corner they stopped.

"Lou'."

"Yeah?"

"Did my eyes see what I thought I just saw back there?" Willie puzzled. "I mean, them folks, after a second or so, they acted polite...they actually *cooperated*. God knows, especially in this neighborhood, everybody's usually uptight, ready to bust you one if you just look at'em the wrong way, but tonight they were different."

"Yeah, strange, won't it? Twas like somethin's come over'em." Louella looked at Willie as he, frowning, scratched his head.

They crossed to the opposite sidewalk and continued walking, passing several shops, followed by rows of look-alike tenements. Near the middle of the next block, a small group clustered in front of a stoop. On its top landing, a woman stood talking to the half circle of listeners below. The speaker was Reverend Blind Mary.

"Ah, wait up, Lou," Willie said. "Let's listen for a couple seconds." They stopped.

"Today," the preacher said, voice stern, "Providence informed me that the time is *finally* upon us. The Miracle Event is all but here, and its site will be revealed to me shortly." A tattered scarf circling her neck, the old woman shivered. "Soon...*very soon*, the child will arrive. So, my brothers and sisters, be ever watchful."

"Lou'."

"Huh?"

"That's the preacher I was telling-ya 'bout -- Reverend Blind Mary."

"So that's her, uh?" Louella whispered, straining her neck to get a better look.

"Now," the evangelist continued, "I must leave and further spread the news." She paused. "Son," she said, speaking to the man beside her, "mind helping me down these steps?"

Doting, her aide guided the sightless woman to the sidewalk.

"Lou', I can't believe what my eyes is seein'. I just *can't believe'm!*"

"What-cha mean?"

"Just don't seem possible!"

"Willie, what're you talking 'bout? "

"That man helping Blind Mary."

"What 'bout'm? Just some kind, caring gentleman doing what the Good Book teach, help the infirmed, the blind."

"Caring? Lou', that's...why that's *Snake*. Snake Johnson!"

"Who?"

"Oh, I forgot, you don't know Snake Johnson. Lou', this morning I learned Snake is probably the worst black heart in DC. Was told him and another thug stole a load-a toys Santa was gonna deliver to poor kids at Christmas. How *low* can one piece of human slime sink? Stealing children's dreams like that. And now what is this hoodlum doing? Look at him, acting like a saint, helping that blind woman as if he was her son. Wonder what got in him? Sure is peculiar."

"Well, lotta peculiar things happening 'round here tonight, Willie, a lot."

"That's for sure."

"Ah, Willie, I betta get home, fast. This pain's killing me."

He studied her eyes; the agony in them was stark and fierce. "Yeah, you right, baby...we betta go."

✳ *Chapter Eighteen*

Minutes later they stood at the intersection of
Seventh and Florida Avenue.
"Willie, I'm gettin' tired, *bone tired*, feel like
I'm 'bout ready to collapse."
"Ah, why don't we step in this diner here?" he
suggested, nodding towards Stoney's Food Paradise.
"About any place, Willie, *any* place will do. I
just need to get off my feet and thaw out a little."
"'Course."
"Besides, maybe inside I can get a glass-a water
and take one-a my pills."
"Good idea."
They entered the neighborhood restaurant.
Fingers of warmth greeted them at the door,
caressed their faces, and soon the numbness in their
cheeks began to thaw.
"Willie, I'm gone go 'head and set down in that
booth over yonder. Mind getting me the water for
my pill?"
"Sure."

Willie walked to the counter.

"Cup-a water, please?"

The waiter frowned. "Ah, water, you say?"

"Yeah, water, cup-a-water."

"You mean, just water? No 'burger? No fries? Onion rings? Nothing, but water?"

"Right."

"I'll...I'll have to check with Mr. Stoney, the owner, 'bout that water. People don't just walk in here and order water." After going to the end of the counter and conferring with the middle-aged man seated behind a cash register, the waiter returned and picked up a paper cup, filled it with water, then sat the container in front of Willie. "Should I charge'm, Mr. Stoney?"

"Naw. It's Christmas, Jason," Mr. Stoney grunted as he rang up a customer's order. "Where's your season spirit? We'll overlook the charge...this time. Day after Christmas though, it'll be business as usual; quarter for the cup, quarter for the water -- no exceptions."

"Yes, sir." The young waiter faced Willie. "Anything else?"

"Naw. And thanks."

"Uh-huh."

Jason eyed the "deadbeat" customer, then began wiping the counter as Willie walked to the booth where Louella waited. "Here's your water," he said, sitting.

"Thanks, baby."

Except for Willie and Louella, the diner was almost empty. Customers who normally ate there at that hour were no doubt outside, and, like others, gazing at the comet. Satisfied the counter was clean, the waiter, yawning, strolled to the window and looked out. "Jason, what's going on out there now?" Mr. Stoney asked.

"Same thing, boss. The sky's lit up, traffic jammed, folks standing 'round staring." Jason scratched his head. "Whole thing sure is mystifying, ain't it, Mr. Stoney?"

"No, not really."

"What-cha mean?"

"Look, son, there's a simple explanation for what's going on tonight."

"There is?"

"Sure. I say what you see in that sky is just one-a them spy satellites or a flying saucer the gov'ment launched."

"Um-m-m. Never thought-a that."

"That's the first thing came to my mind. Gov'ment's tricky, son. Always doing stuff behind our back."

"You might have a point. Still, boss, you gotta admit it's mighty odd. But then, recently all-ya hear in this neighborhood is odd stuff. Guess you heard all that talk about 'The Great Event.'"

"Yeah, I heard."

"Know what a customer told me? He said he thought the comet was tied in with The Great Event, The Miracle."

"*Miracle*?"

"Yes, sir, miracle."

"Is that what folks calling it now?"

"Yes, sir."

"You don't believe that miracle stuff, do you?"

"I'll admit it is kinda hard to swallow."

"But do you believe it?"

"I really don't know what to believe no more, to be frank."

"Well I do. Lemme tell-ya something. All that talk 'bout some *miracle* taking place this Christmas, know what that sound like to me, Jason?"

"No, sir."

"Nothing more miraculous than the gov'ment spreading propaganda, that's all, one-a their cover stories."

"So you think it's just part of some, say, CIA or State Department plot?"

"Exactly."

"Well, whatever it is, Mr. Stoney, that sky's sure lit up tonight, almost bright as day...a sight to see, like...like...God's smiling down on us or what it must have looked like when The Creator said, 'Let there be light.'"

A customer entered. "OK, son, that's enough talk," the owner said, "go on back to your station now. You got work to do."

"Yes, sir." Jason tarried, and, with eyes wide, continued gazing at the sky. "Mr. Stoney, I say if the comet's a sign, it must be a sign for something big, *real big*."

"What-cha say, Jason?"

"Ah, nothing, Mr. Stoney. Just talking to myself."

"Oh."

Louella removed a pill from one of the little packets. She slipped the medicine into her mouth and flushed it down with several gulps of water. After which, she winced.

"What's wrong, pill bitter?" Willie asked.

"Naw."

"What then? More pain?"

"'Fraid so. But the pain this time, Willie, it's...it's different."

"How?"

"It's coming more often, like in waves...each one of 'em a little stronger."

"Stronger, you say?"

"Lots." She looked at him. "Willie, I guess you know what that probably mean."

"You don't have to tell me, Lou'. Come on. This diner, it ain't no place for no woman 'bout to deliver no baby."

They walked to the door and stopped.

"Willie."

"Huh?"

"If the baby start coming when we get home, I want you to step down the hall to Mrs. Hinton's room. She's a midwife and know what to do, that is, if she ain't stoned. She got two kids of her own. 'Course, they don't live with her no more. Court put'em in foster care. That woman stay drunk most of the time."

"Sure hope she ain't drunk tonight."

"Willie, hush, don't even think that."

They walked west on Florida Avenue. For the

first half block, Louella had no trouble keeping abreast of Willie. Gradually, however, her pace slackened. She struggled to match his steps, but couldn't. Panting and clutching her stomach, she stopped.

"More pain, Lou'?"

"'Fraid so. Pill don't seem to be helping none."

"Maybe it ain't had time to work."

"Hope you right 'cause right now, Willie, fireworks are exploding in my belly and my back."

"That bad?"

"Sure is."

"Well, I hope you're gonna be able to hold on, baby; we ain't got far to go now. So hang in there just a little while lon--"

"I'm trying, Willie," she grimaced, "God *knows* I'm *trying*..."

A policeman stood near the corner. As Willie and Louella approached, he studied her face.

"Lady, you look kinda sickly. Need some help?"

"'Preciate it, officer," she said through gritted teeth, "but we live just a block or so 'way. I think I can make it. But it's comforting to know someone, a stranger, is concerned, is caring."

"That's something we *all* need to be, lady...caring. And if we humans can't be that way, especially at Christmas, God help us all."

Whistling, a torrent of wind raced past. Willie slipped his arms around Louella. Half a block later as they reached an alley, another gust exploded, lashing punishment. "Willie, how much farther we gotta go?" Louella asked, eyes closed to shield them from the wind.

"Not far, baby. Not far."

"Thank God."

"Now don't fret, Lou', we gone make it."

Comforted, she nestled her head against his arm.

They had walked another block when Willie said, "Lou', you can open your eyes now."

"Are we home?" she asked, eyelids parting slightly.

"Not yet, but we close. Only 'bout a half block more and we'll be at Fourteenth and Florida. Won't be far then."

When they reached Fourteenth and Florida, they turned left. Soon they'd be home, home, their refuge from coldness and wind -- except, of course, air that hissed through cracks around their window, and drafts slithering under the door. Once in the room, Louella would be, at least, reasonably warm; she could then kick off her shoes, stretch across the bed and wait for the pain to ease.

Moving down Fourteenth Street, they soon discovered not everyone in Northwest DC was intrigued by the comet or the prophesies of a street preacher. A man approached.

"Hey, good people," he grinned, "got'em *all* for-ya tonight. Slammas. Ball bustas. Mary Jane. Speed. Heaven dust. And *dig*, to celebrate the season, I'm offering a special Christmas discount."

Louella and Willie silently walked around the drug dealer.

Straight ahead was the tenement where they lived. Illumination from the comet tinted it an early-dawn yellow. In front of the building, a group of about twenty congregated. None looked at the comet. A few milled on the sidewalk, others in the street near the curb, all forming a circle and staring at something in its center. What the something was Willie and Louella couldn't tell.

"Lou', all them folks, why they just standing there?"

"Beat me."

"Wonder what's going on?"

"I don't know."

"I mean, they just...*staring*? Like they viewing a body at a wake. Why ain't they looking at the comet, like everybody else?"

The couple was now within yards of the mysterious circle. Finally they were able to see what the ring of people stared at.

Louella gasped. "Willie! It *can't* be! No, God! It just...just *can't* be!"

"'Fraid it is, Lou'."

"*Lor-r-r-d,* have mercy!"

On the sidewalk centering the spectators and piled in disarray, sat all the couple's belongings.

"The landlord, he done set our stuff out on the sidewalk." Willie moaned in dismay. "And he did it on Christmas *Eve*, no less! In this freezing weather, we...we been evicted? And to top that off, you 'bout to have your baby."

The scavengers stalking their possessions heard the anguish in the couple's voices. None of the listeners seemed moved; all remained poised, ready to pounce.

A giant of a man strode forward and from the pile snatched a chair, then raced down the sidewalk. Another grabbed a lamp. Rummaging, he hurriedly found its mate, and, with one in each hand, raced away.

Two women tug-a-warred with a toaster.

"That's mine!"

"Like hell!"

"You bitch!"

Releasing the contested booty, the heavier of the two women yanked her competitor's hair.

"Take it from the hussy!" someone yelled.

"Kill'er, kill'er!"

Louella eyed the brawlers and winced. Unable to watch any longer, she looked away, tears trailing down her cheeks. "Willie, they're like...*animals*."

"Come on, Lou', we'd better go."

"Go, Willie? Where to?"

"The first place is upstairs to have a word with that landlord."

"For what? Ain't gone do no good."

"Maybe not, but at least I can give him a piece-a my mind. So come on, Lou'."

"Willie, he's just gonna tell us--"

"Who knows what he'll say, Lou'? Could be he'll let us stay another night. That might be all the time you'll need to have your baby. We got nothing to lose. *Nothing!*"

They mounted the steps leading to the building. The landlord's apartment was on the third floor, just above where Willie and Louella once lived. Panting, Louella said she'd wait in the vestibule. "Sure, Lou'." Seconds later, Willie knocked on the landlord's door.

"Yeah?"

"It's me, Mr. Ferguson...Willie Peterson."

"Oh, you."

"Right."

"And what can I do for you, Willie?"

"Like-ya to explain somethin'."

"Happy to, if I can."

"Mr. Ferguson, did you have to set our stuff out on this, of *all* nights...Christmas Eve? Couldn't you have at least waited till after Christmas?"

"Willie, what else could I do? You people ain't paid a dime in weeks. You didn't leave me no choice."

"Look, I know we fell behind. And Lord knows I don't feel good 'bout that. But you understood why we fell behind. I busted my back on my job. Look, I've always took pride in paying my honest debts, Mr. Ferguson, when I can. But to put me and my wife out *now*, on this holy *night*, when she's 'bout to birth her baby, plus, to make matters worser, when it's as cold as the North Pole outside, and us with no place to go. It ain't...it ain't *human*. Anyway, Mr. Ferguson, you didn't give us no proper notice."

"I sure did. I taped it to your door couple-a days ago."

"Well, I didn't see it."

"I put it up there alright. Guess somebody

must-a ripped it down. Maybe that was their idea of a joke."

"*Some* joke."

"Know what-ya mean. Well, anyway, I hope you find some place to stay."

"It ain't me I'm concerned 'bout, Mr. Ferguson. It's my wife and that baby. Me? I can sleep in a doorway, over a grate, any place. Don't matter. Like I told-ya, she's 'bout to deliver, plus she's sick as a dog. She downstairs now waiting in the vestibule." Willie paused. "Mr. Ferguson."

"Yeah."

"My wife's gotta get to some place to have her baby...fast. And a freezing city sidewalk shouldn't have to be that place."

"I understand, Willie, and I sympathize."

"Mr. Ferguson."

"Yeah."

"I'm wondering, can't-cha find it in your heart to let us stay until...just tomorrow night? I figure she'll have the baby tonight sometime, early tomorrow at the latest. Then, you got my word, we'll be outta here for good."

"Wish I could accommodate you, Willie, really do, but I can't. You see, I've gone far as I can."

"*One more night*, Mr. Ferguson, what difference could that make?"

"Like I said, Willie, I can't. The new tenant for your place say he's gonna move in tomorrow, early...at dawn. And I can't have him putting his stuff in a room with blood and birth water splattered over everything. Even if you clean it up with

ammonia, the place'll still stink. You wouldn't wanna
move in no 'partment like that, yourself. Nobody
would. So, I'm sorry." He paused, "Willie?"
  "Yeah."
  "You still there?"
  "I'm still here."
  "Thought for a second you'd gone."
  "Gone, Mr. Ferguson?"
  "Yeah."
  "Where to?"
  "I...I...I don't know, but ah, like I said, I can't
help you."
  "I heard-cha."
  "Hope you understand."
  "On a freezing night like this, Mr. Ferguson,
with my wife 'bout to give birth and us with no
place to go, well, understanding's kinda hard to do."
  "Ah, anyway, I trust your wife'll have her baby
in some warm, safe place. Ah, tell her I said that."
  "So you want me to tell-er that, uh?"
  "Yeah, if you don't mind."
  "I'll...I'll be sure to pass on your...*good wishes*,
Mr. Ferguson."
  "'Preciate it."
  Heart pounding, stomach churning in fear,
Willie plodded down the stairs. What to do, he
puzzled. What to do about everything. He thought
about Louella...her delivery...her nausea...her pain.
He wondered in what direction he should, could
turn? Who to see? Where to go?
  He never felt so helpless for he knew no one to
see, no place to go. Go to a hospital perhaps? There

he and Louella would surely be turned away, if not removed at gun point.

"Ah, your health insurance, sir, with what company are you enrolled? Blue Cross? Safety Net? The exclusive Hospital Supreme? Oh-h-h-h? None of these, you say? Um...I...I...see. I take it you plan to pay in cash. No checks. Cash only...up front."

Willie of course had neither hospital insurance, nor cash. How could a scavenger of trash bins afford health insurance? And as for "up front cash?" He couldn't pay "rear end" money, let alone the "up front" kind.

If the truth were known, he'd be unable to come up with taxi fare to the nearest hospital if obstetricians there agreed to deliver Louella's baby for free.

Borrow the money from a bank perhaps? Unthinkable. Seeing him, officials would chuckle. How could someone like Willie Peterson have the *gall* to apply for a loan? In spite of their slick ads, banks, he knew, "as policy," never lent money to those needing it. On the other hand, if he were a millionaire loan applicant, he'd be greeted with warm arms and open vaults.

He had no idea what he'd tell Louella. Should he tell her she couldn't have her baby under normal conditions like other women -- in a certified delivery room, hers and the child's progress monitored by state-of-the-art equipment? He shrugged. Why tell her that? These things she already knew.

When he reached the vestibule he found his wife, eyes closed, leaning against the wall, her face a study in anguish.

"Lou'. Is your pain as bad as your expression say it is?"

"No."

"That's good."

"It's worser, Willie, much worser. My face, no face, can't really show the hurt inside."

"Well, hate to say this, but I'm 'fraid you gonna have to hang on a little longer."

"I only hope God will give me the strength, Willie...just hope He will. Now, tell me, what'd the landlord say?"

"Said he was sorry and all but ain't nothing more he can do."

"I figgered he'd say that."

"Me too, but I *had* to at least try, Lou'. And oh yeah, he said to tell-ya he hope you find some warm place where you can have your baby."

"Did he really have nerve enough to say that, Willie?" Both shrugged in disbelief, then headed for the door, hand in hand. "Willie," Louella said, "I got a feeling it ain't gonna be long before the baby will be com--"

"I know, Lou. I know." At the door, she stopped. "Come on, Lou' let's get outta here."

"And go where?"

"I don't know. But we gone find a place... *somewhere.*"

"Willie, I'm scared!"

"You wouldn't be human if you won't."

"I'm real scared!"

"Lou'."

"What?"

"You ain't the *only* one scared. But like I said, we'll find a place for you. It'll turn up, you'll see."

"It'd betta, Willie...and soon, 'cause the pain is coming faster and faster."

He slipped his hand under her elbow, then guided her outside. Leading her where? He didn't have a clue.

✳ *Chapter Nineteen*

When the couple reached the sidewalk, they turned right, circumventing thrashing bodies and flying fists, as brawlers battled over ownership of Willie and Louella's belongings. Once they passed the melee, they headed west towards Fourteenth and U.

A block later, Louella gasped, "Willie, I gotta stop!"

"You...OK?"

"It's just that I'm so tired, Willie, and the pain's so bad."

"Wanna take 'nother pill?"

"Naw."

"Why not?"

"Ain't been too long since I took the last. Take too many, I could get worser than I am. Besides, might harm the baby."

"Hadn't thought-a that. Ah, Lou.'"

"Yeah."

"I wanna tell-ya somethin', somethin' I'm sure you don't know, fact, most women probably don't. Why not? Well, because God made women women, and men men. They different. Listen, Lou', seeing you in agony as you is now and not being able to help, is, well, it's something I, as a man, don't handle too graceful. It rip me apart inside, make me feel...I'm less than a man, knowing there ain't *nothing* I can do for my woman. Make me feel *helpless*. And men don't like to feel that way. Lou', you...understand what I'm trying to say, though I know I ain't saying it too good?"

"I think I get the general idea, Willie. But, like you say, being a woman, there're things I'll never be able to see through a man's eyes. But I want-ya to understand one thing, I do 'preciate your concern 'bout me. I really do."

"Lou', for a man the hardest part is feeling so...*helpless*."

"But, Willie, you *is* helping."

"I am? How?"

"You...show you *care*. That's helping. And you're *here*, when I need-cha. That's helping, too."

"Still, Lou', the *man* in me keep nagging that I oughtta be doing *more*."

She caressed his hand. The gesture calmed him. She was happy it did, though the truth was, she hadn't fully understood all he'd tried to tell her -- and probably never would.

They leaned into the wind, both hoping it would subside. It didn't. To escape its sting, they stepped into the recessed entrance of Tessa's Beauty Shop, which provided a partial barrier.

"Willie," Louella said following a pause, "wonder what our baby's gonna be like?"

"Who knows? Having a kid is like rolling dice, Lou'."

"Think he'll ever 'preciate what we went through to bring'm in the world?"

"Doubtful. Children, old folks say, never do. So I figger the best we can hope for is, when he grow up, we might get a 'thank-ya'...might."

"Anyway, hope he turn out OK, not like them folks back there fighting over our stuff, acting like animals."

"Lou', listen. As for our kid, I don't think you got a thing to worry 'bout, not one thing."

"Why you say that?"

"Look, any child *you* birth, Lou', he can't possibly turn out bad."

She said nothing. Finally. "Willie."

"Yeah."

"Thank you, baby. You always seem to know what it is I needs to hear."

Gradually the wind's velocity decreased, its howl modulating into a whistle. Both had walked a half block when Louella stopped, then clutched her belly, and, like a spring-loaded hinge, lurched, then quivered. "*Good God!*" she screamed.

"What's the matter!"

"Willie!"

"You don't have to yell, Lou'. I'm still here 'side-ya."

"The pain! It's awful! I gotta go somewhere, I

gotta get inside outta this bitter cold. I gotta..."
"And you *will*, Lou', believe me, you will."
"Please, God," she moaned, "don't let my baby be born on no sidewalk in this freezing weather! *Please!*"
"Lou'--"
"Willie, what we gone do, where we gonna go?"
"I don't know, Lou', I... Ah, gimme a second to think. Let me get my thoughts together." Willie frantically looked around as he spoke.
"Hurry, Willie, please *hurry!*"
They were within a half block of Fourteenth and U. Near the intersection were several bars and grills -- The Silver Slipper, Moody's Haunt, The Golden Jackass. None, of course, was a substitute for what Louella needed, a maternity ward. All were businesses, there for one purpose: to generate profit. If Louella and Willie asked for shelter at any of them, even temporary shelter -- just long enough for her to have her baby -- both knew what the answer would be: a scowl and a door slammed in their faces.
Willie realized that having her baby represented the most glorious moment of Louella's less-than-glorious life, the validation of her identity as a woman. Being obliged -- and on Christmas Eve no less -- to give birth on a frozen slab of concrete was a thought that sickened him, as surely as it did Louella.
He imagined her on her back near the curb, whistling winds sweeping litter past. The image was unsettling; it fractured his perception of self. Self as

husband. Father. Protector. *Man.* He envisioned his wife in the delivery position, back pressing the sidewalk, legs spread. Passersby would gawk at the "disgraceful spectacle."

"Willie, what in the world are we gonna do?"

"Just hang on, baby, hear? Hang..."

He scanned the opposite side of the street; there he saw endless rows of tenements, some boarded, all drab. None showed signs of life. Windows, darkened. Shades, drawn. Willie focused on the corner tenement. There, lights, though dim, glowed in every window. Occasionally its front door opened and someone exited.

"Lou'."

"What?"

"That house yonder, the end one. We...we can try there."

She looked at the designated tenement, then at Willie. "But that's the *crack house*, Willie, the one folks talk so much 'bout?"

"I know, Lou'. But, with you in pain and all, and the baby 'bout to be born, what choice we got?"

Louella lowered her head...and voice. "On second thought, Willie, why *not* that house? As much pain as I'm in, that place is beginning to look more and more like, not what it is, but a...*palace*."

❋ *Chapter Twenty*

They stood facing the scarred front door of the notorious crack house. In a window to the right, a sickly Christmas wreath hung, reminding Willie of a corpse suspended on a gallows. Little of the ornament's plastic "greenery" remained. The tiny candle centering the wreath was twisted and held in place with tape. The bulb was broken and all but the base was missing. Willie glanced at the pathetic adornment, then knocked.

Soon, the door opened. A middle aged man in a tattered sweater towered before the couple. With a scowl and a grunt, he greeted the visitors. "Yeah?"

"Ah," Willie hesitated, "ah--"

"That's be ten bills if you want a needle, nine if you brought your own. Time limit, half hour. No exceptions!"

"Wait."

"For what?"

"You don't understand."

"What's to understand? You heard my prices,

didn't-ya?"

"Yeah, but--"

"What's the problem?"

"We ain't here for that."

"You ain't? So what-cha here for? You house hunting or something? Selling Girl Scout cookies maybe?" Before Willie could answer. "Don't tell me...no, don't tell me. I think I already know. You two are a couple of undercover cops. Right? Had a feeling you might be. Usually I can spot'em a block away."

"No, no, no," Willie sputtered as he waved his hands, "...ain't like that!" The man's demeanor changed after he probed Willie's eyes. Apparently there was something in them that convinced him the couple weren't cops. "Ah, look, ah...we got a problem."

"Everybody walk through that door say the *same* thing." The man folded his arms over his massive chest. "What you...*claim* is your problem?"

"Mista, my wife, she's nine months pregnant, could deliver any minute."

"So? What's that gotta do with the price of tea in China?"

"*Please*, lemme finish."

"OK, but make it snappy!"

"Sure. See, my back was busted in a accident; I can't hold no steady, good-paying job. For a living, I collect junk. My wife and me need a place -- *bad*. Landlord, he set our stuff out on the sidewalk tonight. Everything we owned's gone -- thieves went wild. My wife, she need some place outta this weather where she can have her baby. We gotta find it...fast. And I mean *fast.*"

"Don't know who been talking to you, but this house sure ain't the kinda place you looking for. True, I run a service business...but, ah, not the maternity kind...if you get my drift."

"I get it, but that ain't the point."

"Then what is the point?"

"The point is, it's cold as Alaska out here, I'm freezing, she's freezing, and her baby's 'bout to be born...maybe, as we speak." Louella grasped Willie's arm and pressed closer. Suddenly her body trembled. "And me and my wife, we pray to God our child ain't gonna have to draw his first breath on some filthy sidewalk. That's the point."

"Um-m-m-m. So, you claim she's pregnant and in labor, huh?" The man eyed Louella. "Well-l-l," he grunted, "look like you might be telling the truth...*might* be." The shooting gallery operator lowered his hand and placed it on the belly of the alleged mother-to-be. "Sure 'nough *feel* real all right."

"Mista, I wouldn't lie to-ya, believe me."

"Wouldn't, uh? 'Round here, folks say that *all* the time, then they tell me a lie. It's just that I don't want nobody sashaying in here feeding me no con story. Know what I'm saying?"

"Yes, sir."

"Well, at least you understand that much. So...she need a place to have her baby, uh?"

"Yes, sir."

"Well, and this goes against my better

judgment, but tell-ya what I'll do. Gonna let you people stay. But I want both of you to understand one thing. You ain't gonna turn this place into no permanent residence. Get that?" Willie nodded that he did. "If she ain't delivered by tomorrow noon, tomorrow evening at the latest, out you go, bag and baggage. Make myself clear?"

"Yes, sir. Ah...one other thing."

"Yeah?"

"Like I told-ya, I don't have no money for no doctor, and I sure don't know how to deliver a baby. So when it come, I ain't gonna know what to do."

"Can't help you there. Midwifing, well, that ain't exactly my line." The host scratched his head. "Um-m-m, wait a minute. Just had a thought. 'Sweet' Lucy Hanson, she's back there in the room next to where you'll be. Sweet was once a nurse before the monkey mugged her -- good one, too. Anyway, she's back there. You might ask her to help-ya, that is, if she ain't too wasted. Knowing Sweet as I do, she's probably skydiving near Jupiter by now. That woman's a *sad* case. Come from a fine family, she did. Like I said, you might try her."

"Thanks."

"By the way...what'd you say your name is?"

"I didn't, but it's Willie...Willie Peterson. And this here's my wife...Louella."

"Pleasure to make your 'quaintance, m'am," the host smiled -- for the first time -- then nodded respectfully.

"Same here."

"My name's Tony Red...Tony Lewis Red.

Most folks in the neighborhood call me 'Chicago Red' or just plain 'Red.' Either'll do.

"Anyway, Willie, as I was about to say, I kinda understand what you're going through. Won't too long ago I was a first-time father myself -- *scared to death*. Ah, don't mind me saying so, m'am," Red added, turning to Louella, "you're the spitting image of my late wife, Martha -- God rest her soul. Seeing you, well, sorta took me back...to better days, before I got into this, ah...profession." Red paused, transported it seemed, to a happier time. "Anyway," he said, "like I told-ya, Willie, after your wife, I mean, Mrs. Peterson, has her baby -- by no later than tomorrow evening -- you folks'll have to go."

"We understand."

"Good, 'cause you gotta realize one thing: I run a business here. And business is business."

"That's something my landlord taught us tonight, Mr. Red. Sad we had to learn the lesson on a freezing Christmas Eve."

"Yeah, 'tis," Red shrugged, "but that's the way it go sometimes. Christmas to some folks don't mean *nothing*. Just another number on a calendar. A time to shop department store sales, or lay around the house watching football games. Beyond that, to some folks the day ain't got no meaning. Anyway, the toilet's the first door on the left. And your room is near the end of the hall, on the right. I say 'room.' I don't really mean that. It's more like a...closet with a window. Seldom rent it except when things get busy, which tonight they sure ain't."

"Well, it's Christmas Eve," Willie said, "which

might explain the slow business." Another contraction assaulted and Louella tensed.

"Might."

"Could be most folks are home sharing Christmas charity," Willie said. "And speaking of Christmas charity, Mr. Red, it's good to know people like you *still* believe in it. I mean, taking us in the way you did, us being strangers and all. Ain't everybody who'd do that." Seemingly embarrassed by Willie's gratitude, the crack house operator fidgeted. "Tell-ya the truth, Mr. Red, we didn't think you'd do it."

"Didn't, uh."

"No, sir."

"Well, it's kinda funny, ain't it?"

"What?"

"How you think you know somebody, but more often than not, you don't."

"Yeah, it is funny."

"Sometimes I wonder if anybody know anybody else, or just think they do? I mean...really know'm. Anyway, like I said, your room's down the hall there." Willie and Louella turned. "Now," Red added, clearing his throat, "I don't want word leaked that I let you folks stay here. I ain't generally known as the kinda man who'd do a thing like that. It's just that your wife, well, to tell you the truth, she reminded me so much of Martha..." A smile creased Red's lips. Then, as if suddenly aware he was smiling, he scowled. "Not a word. Ya hear?"

"Yes, sir."

The hall was narrow. Litter covered much of

the floor -- styrofoam cups, soda straws, crumpled paper bags, most discolored by vintage dust. Very little wallpaper remained. Surviving strips were dingy, artifacts of happier times when the tenement and neighborhood enjoyed prosperity. Near the baseboard, someone using a Magic Marker had scrolled a series of loops; above these were the words "Cocaine, Hell's Whore." The bright red lettering contrasted the wall's drabness.

A little window looked down from the end of the hall. Two curtains partially covered it, one chestnut, the other burgundy, both threadbare and somber. There were no pictures on the walls, no clocks or posters...nothing. A bare bulb hung from the ceiling, its glow casting pale shadows.

Willie and Louella approached a room they thought was theirs, but wasn't. They looked inside. A little lamp was on the floor, beside it, a gaunt man fingering a syringe. Silent, he stared at the couple.

On the opposite side of the room a woman in her early twenties sat, back angled against the wall. "Don't take my baby," she babbled, "not at Christmas. I've changed, I've found The Savior, gonna stay clean now...I swear to God, I'll stay clean."

Willie and Louella finally found their room. Though smaller, it was similar to the one they'd looked in. Except for a few rags piled in a corner and several discarded syringes scattered here and there, the floor was bare. Not so the walls. All were covered with graffiti.

"Sorta chilly in here, ain't it, Willie?"

"Yeah it is, but it ain't really too bad."

"Compared to outside, you right."

"We just need a little time to let our bodies thaw some, Lou."

Willie walked to the radiator and touched it -- lukewarm. Smell of urine perfumed the room, the stench strongest near the radiator, as was the musty odor of aged dust. On the wall beneath the window someone had scribbled, "Our Father, Crack Cocaine, give us this day...please!"

"You wanna lay down now, Lou'?"

"Yeah, I think I'd betta."

"Be careful, don't step on one-a them nails sticking up. And watch out for splinters, too."

"Sure."

"Last thing you need is ptomaine."

"The *very* last, Willie."

A syringe lay near Louella's feet. Willie kicked it, skidding it into a corner.

He took off his coat. Louella, hers. His he spread on the floor, making a pallet.

"Lou, want me to help you down?"

"Naw, that's OK, I...I think I can manage." Once she had stretched out on the pallet, he placed her coat over her, then, slipping under it, snuggled beside her, circling his arm around her waist and feeling her shiver.

"Are you...are you all right, baby?"

"I'll be fine. I just need a little more time to warm up, that's all."

Minutes later, they heard footsteps in the hall.

"Ah, you leaving, Carlos?" Red yelled from the

other end of the corridor.

"Yeah."

"Well, till next time, good buddy."

"Next time, Red?"

"Yeah...as usual."

"Red, for me, there ain't gonna be no next time.'"

"Aw, come on, Carlos. It's Christmas...cheer up. No more that gloomy talk 'bout taking your life. You fret too much."

"Do I?" Carlos opened the front door.

"Yeah, ya do."

"Been nice knowing you, Red."

"Like I said: see-ya next time, Carlos."

"Goodbye, Red."

After hesitating, Carlos stepped into Christmas Eve's darkness.

"Huh," Red grunted, hurrying down the hall, "wonder why he'd leave that door open?" Red closed it against the frigid night.

Willie and Louella, silent, stared into the grayness of their room. "Lou' how's the baby doing?"

"Much betta then us."

"What-cha mean by that?"

"He's inside me, Willie, away from" -- she scanned the room -- "...all of this."

Later, head resting against his shoulder, Louella was unaware of the increased traffic in the hall, as more and more customers came and went, for she had fallen asleep. Several minutes later Willie dozed off, too, but not for long.

"Willie!" Louella suddenly exploded, her elbow jabbing his side. "Willie!"

"What...what, Lou'? Pain start again?"

"Yes! The baby...I can feel it coming!"

He popped to his feet. "Just be calm. I'll scoot and get the lady in the next room. She'll know what to do." He darted into the hall. Mini-seconds later, he, panting, stood in the adjoining room looking down at Sweet Lucy Hanson, who, like a corpse, sprawled on the floor. Beside her lay a threadbare army field jacket. A syringe angled from her arm. "Wake up!" Willie shook her. "*Wake up!*" Again he shook, harder. "Lady--"

"Huh? What's the..." Lucy mumbled, eyes glazed marbles, "what's...what's the matter?"

"Come on, lady, please, *wake up!*"

"Who...who're you?"

"Willie Peterson. Now wake up! Need your help!"

"Me? Help? Nobody ever calls on me for help. Help who? Where?"

"My wife, she's in the next room 'bout to have a baby. Red said you know how to deliver'em, that you used to be a nurse, and a good one, too."

"Red said that?"

"Yeah."

"Well, he's telling the truth, I used to be a nurse all right. Registered. Then again...I used to be a l*ot* of things. *Used to be.*"

"*Please*...won't-cha help us?"

"Where...where'd you say your wife is?"

"In the next room."

Sweet Lucy rubbed her eyes. "Ah, gimme a second," she slurred. "Lemme see if I can pull myself together and get up."

"Wait!" Willie said, "don't move."

"Why?"

He eased the syringe from her arm and tossed it to the floor. "There. Now lemme help-ya up."

Sweet nudged his hand aside. "I can do it myself...I...I think." The former nurse wobbled to her feet, stumbled to the door, then leaned against its frame.

"Listen," she said, "want you to go to Red, and tell'm to give you a butcher knife. On second thought, he probably doesn't have one. Ah, ask him to lend you that switchblade he carries. Yeah, that'll do. The fact he once almost stabbed a man to death with it won't make no difference now."

"Anything else?"

"Yes."

"What?"

"See if he has any towels. If not, we'll have to make do."

"That all?"

"For now, yes."

"Ah...ah, wanna thank-ya, Miss Hanson, really 'preciate your help."

"What did you say?"

"Said I 'preciate your help.'"

"No, before that. Did you call me...*Miss...Miss* Hanson?"

"That's your name, ain't it? Or is it Mrs.?"

"No, Miss," Sweet Lucy stared into blankness.

"Lord, when was the last time," she sighed, shaking her head, "the last time somebody put a handle on...*my* name? I'd forgotten how it sounded."
"Anyway, like I said, thank-ya, Miss Hanson."
"Don't thank me, Willie."
"Why not?"
"Because I should be...thanking...*you*."
"For what?"
"For...helping me to find something that I... lost...long ago."
"I don't understand."
"Well, if it make you feel better, Willie, I don''t fully understand it myself. But that doesn't matter. Anyway," she added, picking up the field jacket and slipping into it, "hurry and get those things for me."
"Yes, m'am. Be right back."
Willie bolted down the hall. Red didn't have a butcher knife, so he lent him his switchblade. The weapon measured nearly eight inches. Willie wondered how the victim that the knife's owner once stabbed with it could have survived. The dagger-like instrument was obviously designed to end life, not inaugurate it.
When Willie reentered the room, Sweet Lucy was on her knees in front of Louella who, legs spread, now writhed in pain. "My Lord, the pain...oh-h-h my God!" Willie handed the switchblade to Sweet, then told her Red didn't have any towels.
"No towels, uh? Well...how about handing me one of those," she said, pointing to a pile of rags in the far corner. "Pick the cleanest of the lot."

"Sure."

"When I tell you," Sweet said to Louella, "I want you to push, understand, I mean *really* push. Give it everything."

Willie returned with the cleanest of the dirt-soiled cloths and stood beside the midwife.

"Drop it here on her breast," Sweet said. Willie did. With her palm, Lucy wiped perspiration from Louella's forehead. "Ah, you might want to step outside," Sweet suggested. "Seeing this sorta thing makes some men a little...queasy. And I wouldn't want to see you...puke on your wife."

Willie left.

✳ *Chapter Twenty-One*

As soon as he stepped over the threshold, Willie's composure faltered. Fidgeting, he stuffed his hands in his pockets, jerked them out, then reinserted them. He didn't know when or how they escaped, only that they did, then hung tensely by his sides.

To calm himself, he paced the hall several times, on each trek striding more rapidly. During the third excursion, he stopped at the front door, inhaled deeply, saturating his lungs, then exhaled, jetting air through tense nostrils.

Louella exploded a shriek. "My Lord, I..."

Her voice ripped his nerves like buzz saws. "The pain, Jesus help me, the pain..." Frustrated, Willie slammed his fists into the wall. "Bam!" The release of energy lessened his anxiety. Calmer, he slid back the curtain covering the little window in the front door and looked out.

Abruptly his eyes widened and his jaw sagged. In front of the house, almost as far as could be seen, hundreds of people massed -- easily between eight and nine hundred. People were everywhere. Overflowing sidewalks. Carpeting streets. Shoulder to shoulder they stood -- men, women, old, young, some richly attired, others dressed like tramps. Willie scanned to the right -- there were too many bodies to count. To the left -- a similar number. All silent, staring, nearly motionless, as if welded in place.

"What the *hell's* going on out there?" Red growled, hurrying down the stairs.

"Beats me."

"I was up in the john when I glanced out the window and saw all these *folks*..." Buckling his belt, Red stood beside Willie, and, like him, gazed out.

"Just seem to be a lotta folks standing and staring and saying nothing, Mr. Red."

"But why? What's up?"

"Your guess's as good as mine."

"Hope not, Willie, 'cause mine ain't didley: I ain't got the faintest."

Willie studied the throng, gradually directing his attention to a single spectator, a woman directly in front of the house -- Reverend Blind Mary.

Snake stood beside the preacher, and, like others, stared at the house. Soon, Mary stepped forward, tottered. Snake steadied the old woman. The hoodlum then led her towards the house.

"Know that lady coming this way?" Willie asked.

"Don't everybody in Northwest Washington? That's Reverend Blind Mary. But why would a good and righteous woman like her be coming to a place like--"

"Don't know," Willie said, then paused. "Umm-m, wait a minute."

"What?"

"Just thought...maybe...maybe she's coming here because of the Miracle Child."

"Because of what?"

Willie shrugged. "Ah, nothing. Just a passing thought. Probably don't mean a thing."

"Oh."

The evangelist and her escort stood before the front door. Snake raised his hand to knock. Before he could, Red opened the door. "How are you, Mary?" he greeted.

The preacher's face was a sunburst of joy. "How am I? At the moment, I'm floating on clouds! Feeling better than I've *ever* felt in all my days." She steadied herself, then said, "Ah, that voice I just heard, it sounds like somebody I once knew."

"You're right, Mary."

"Is that you, Red?"

"The same. Been a while, hasn't it?"

"Has that. Why, the last time we talked you had a janitor's job cleaning the dorm where I lived."

"You got a good memory for voices."

"Then one day you disappeared, Red, never saw you again. What happened?"

"Well, there was sickness in my family, Mary; mamma had cancer. Hospital bills, sky high. I needed money -- fast. So, I got it the only way I knew. Anyway, Momma, she's OK now."

"God is merciful, isn't he, Red? And you, what

have you been doing all these years?"

"What we all do, Mary. Trying to stay alive in a cesspool of sharks. But enough 'bout me. Tell me, what brings you...ah, guess what I really mean is...why are all these people congregated in front of my house."

"Red, they're here to welcome him who'll rehabilitate Christmas."

"But, why here?"

"Earlier tonight, I announced the great event would take place this Christmas Eve, and later, that it'd happen at *this* address. Like me, they're here to bear witness to--" The cry of a baby interrupted. "The child, I hear *the child*!" Mary's eyes beamed. "Quick, where is the baby?"

"Just down the hall," Willie said.

"Take me to him, *please*."

"'Course."

Willie led the way. When they entered the room, Louella lay on her back, legs spread, blood and birth fluid puddling the pallet. Sweet Lucy sat beside the new mother. The midwife had wrapped the baby in the tattered army field jacket she'd worn. Beaming, she cuddled the newborn, occasionally kissing its cheeks, and, eyes wide, smiling at the new life she helped launch. "It's a boy," she said to the father.

"Is...he," Willie stammered, "is he...OK?"

"Perfectly healthy. All parts accounted for and in working order."

"*Thank God!*" Willie heaved. "Thank God."

"Please," Mary interrupted, "allow me to touch

him."

"Of course," Sweet said, elevating the baby.

Snake guided Mary's hand. When she touched the newborn, the preacher glowed. "My mission," she sighed, as if relieved of a burden, "is ended. At last, Yuletide will have a fresh beginning."

She bowed her head. "Father, she prayed, "he has come, and now I must depart." She paused. "Master, your voice, I hear it calling my name, summoning me, and I will abide by your will." Both puzzled by Mary's strange prayer, Red and Willie stared at each other. "For above all, thy will must be done. Amen." Mary turned to Snake. "Son, will you kindly lead me to my room. Before sunrise, I must begin my return journey home."

"Yes, m'am."

Snake escorted the old woman from the room. Watching them, Willie recalled Mary's strange prayer, and wondered what it meant.

✳ *Chapter Twenty-Two*

Outside, near the intersection of Fourteenth and U, Officer Topper Grove depressed the brake pedal of his police cruiser. The vehicle eased to a stop, blocked by an impenetrable wall of spectators clogging the street. He switched off the ignition, got out, snaked his way to the crowd's perimeter and approached a middle-aged woman.

"Ah, excuse me, m'am, but what going on?" The matron turned, stared at the law official, but said nothing. "What's the problem here?" Again she looked at him as if he were invisible, his words remnants of a forgotten tongue.

Frowning, the officer turned to his right. "Pardon, sir," he said, addressing a man in his twenties, "but ah, why're all these people loitering on this corner?"

The male spectator's response duplicated the woman's -- silence and a blank stare. Hurrying, Officer Grove returned to his cruiser, entered it, then flipped on the car radio. "Topper Grove here."

"Yeah, Top'," a female voice crackled from the speaker. "Rita, lemme speak to the cap'n, will-ya?"

"Sure thing. Ah, what's up, Top'?"

"Can't say for sure, but I think we might have a serious situation up here at Fourteenth and U. Anyway, put the cap'n on -- quick."

"'Course. Cap'n', it's for you. Topper."

"Yeah, Top', Captain Timpson here. What-cha got?"

"Chief, there're about eight hundred people congregated in front of this crack house up here at Fourteenth and U, and--"

"Eight hundred, you say?"

"Probably more."

"Well what're they doing? Rioting? Looting? Burning? What?"

"That's just it, Chief. The darndest thing! They're not doing anything, not saying anything either. I asked what was going on, nobody'd answer, not a word. They just stand and stare at that crack house...like, like they're in some sorta...*trance*."

"And you say just standing is all they're doing?"

"Right."

"Look, Top', I can't believe that eight hundred people would gather in front of the worst human *sewer* in DC and nothing illegal is goin' on. Something is happening; the question is what. Trust me, they're up to no good, Top', and I'm counting on you to go in that house and find out what it is. Read me?"

"Ten four. But I'll need backup, Chief. Certainly you don't expect me to just walk in that damn garbage heap by myself."

"'Course not! Look, you'll get backup -- and lots of it. I'll dispatch my best team, armed to the teeth: tear gas, semiautomatics, the whole nine yards. In that neighborhood we'll need all the fire power we can muster. Soon as the team arrives, Top', I want you to bust in that house and check it out, *every inch*. Then get back to me and let me know what's going on in there." Long pause. "Top'."

"Yeah, Chief."

"I think we got ourselves a biggie this time, real big." The Chief's excitement was evident by his rapid breathing.

"My gut feeling exactly."

"Wouldn't surprise me if some terrorist group is behind the whole thing, plotting to topple the government or something."

"Think so?"

"Certain of it. Like I say, I'll dispatch your backup, pronto. OK? Meanwhile, I'll be standing by for your call."

"Sure thing, Chief."

Topper cradled the microphone, then stared ahead at the panorama of people. Everyone seemed oblivious of either him or his patrol car; their gaze was riveted on the Fourteenth and U tenement.

Minutes later, the scream of sirens echoed the neighborhood. Brakes screeched. Cruisers slammed to a halt. Car doors swung open. Officers poured into view. Double-timing, they moved into formation, snapping weapons to the ready position. Tear gas canisters strapped to their belts, all wore black jump suits and body armor. Each carried an AR-15 semiautomatic. In a wedge formation, they cleared a path to where Topper waited.

He and the team commander chatted briefly, then Topper joined the unit as it advanced towards the crack house, moving cautiously, as if anticipating an imminent attack.

"Stand 'side!"

"Make way! Make way!"

"Move! Move!"

Spectators complied to the orders given. None, however, seemed intimidated. When the SWAT team reached the sidewalk, two officers, weapons at the ready, pivoted. Both glared at the crowd.

"Officer Durrell!" barked the commander.

"Ready, sir."

"Officer Sanchez."

"Ready, sir."

The named officers peeled from the formation and, quick-timing, assumed posts on either side of the tenement's front door, then faced the crowd.

"Click."

"Click."

Both disengaged their weapons' safeties.

"Lock and load!" the leader barked.

"Snap!"

"Snap!"

"Rounds chambered, sir!"

"Rounds chambered, sir!"

"Stand by! And fire on my command!"

An hour later, Officer Grove trudged back to his cruiser. Sighing, he plopped into the driver's seat, picked up the microphone and flipped its switch. "Chief."

"Yeah."

"Topper here."

"Quick, how many more men are we gonna need!"

"Chief, you--"

"Just contacted Prince George County PD, and they can let us have twenty men."

"I don't think you understand."

"Cap'n' Berry over in Montgomery County says he can spare about ten."

"Like I'm trying to say, Chief, you don't understand."

"Understand? What's to understand, Top'? You *did* bust in that crack house, didn't you?"

"Just like you told me."

"So what'd you find? 'Street sweepers?' AK-47s? Hand grenades?"

"No, Chief, I--"

"Well...*what*? Stashes of heroin, maybe?"

"Look, we went in there and searched that place with a fine tooth comb, basement to attic, *every inch*, and, guess what, no dope, bombs, guns, nothing."

"I can't believe this!"

"Joint's as clean as a baby's butt. Either they didn't sell drugs there, or they got rid of the stuff before we swooped in. Either way, the bottom line's the same, zilch."

"I will be damn. You mean, you didn't find a thing, not even a Saturday night special?"

"'Bout the closest we came to a weapon was a switchblade I saw laying on the floor. True, it was illegal length, but hardly worth a bust, not when there's so much more *serious* crime in this neighborhood."

"So tell me, Top'."

"Yeah?"

"What the hell *did* you find that explains why on a blistering cold Christmas Eve like this, eight hundred people would gather in front of *all* places, a damn crack house? What?"

"Chief."

"Yeah, Top'."

"Like I said, I didn't find a thing, except filth and a few half stoned junkies mumbling outta their heads."

"And that was it?"

"That was it. No, one other thing, something... strange, chief."

"What?"

"Well, we busted in one of the rooms, weapons drawn and shouting 'Police! Raid! Hands up!' As it turned out, our automatic weapons were trained on, of all things, a mother setting on the floor cuddling her newborn baby. So new, it hadn't been cleaned up yet.

"Seeing her and the child, the SWAT team froze. Chief, we felt like *damn fools*. There we were, a squad of linebacker types with enough fire power to blast hell out of a Chinese combat platoon, and all of it trained on what? A mother and her baby? *Some* threat, uh? Anyway, the mother looked up at us and--"

"Bet she was scared to death, right?"

"She might have been, but she sure didn't show it. For someone looking at the death end of an arsenal of cocked AR-15s, I've never seen anybody more composed. It was as if *she* was the one in command, chief, not us. As if we only had guns -- she, something more...*powerful.*"

"What'd she say?"

"'Merry Christmas,' she smiled. 'And may its love and peace be with you...always.' Then, after kissing her baby, she asked one of the officers if he'd be kind enough to put down his weapon for a second and hand her a rag that lay in the corner. He did, and she dabbed blood from her baby, then continued cuddling it, just like we weren't there -- paying no attention to our AR-15s, all cocked and ready to blow her brains out...as if they were toys, and we were misguided little boys, who didn't understand a thing."

"Um-m-m-m."

"And oh yes, you'll never guess who was in the room with the mother."

"Who?"

"Sweet Lucy Hanson. You know Sweet, don't-cha?"

"Me and every cop in DC."

"Wait'll you hear this. I learned that Sweet was the one who delivered the baby."

"You're joking!" the Chief said.

"I didn't believe it either. Couldn't believe that for once, instead-a shoplifting or conning, and a little of everything in between, Sweet did something redeeming."

"Never thought I'd see the day, Top'. *Never!*"

"Anyway, a few seconds later, the swat team put the safeties back on their weapons, and, heads bowed in shame, we left. What else could we do, Chief? Bust a mother for wishing us love and a merry Christmas, or for cuddling her newborn, or giving birth in a crack house on Christmas Eve? Or maybe we could've collared Sweet for delivering the child? All big time felonies, uh, Chief?

"Course, if you want me to, I'll go back in there and bust a couple of those groggy junkies we found. Is that what you want, chief?"

"Naw, no need for all that. Still, Top', nothing you've said explains why hundreds of people stood in freezing temperatures staring like zombies at a crack house. Nothing."

"You're right, but this might help. Officer Percy Durrell told me as I was making my way back to the cruiser, that if I wanted to find out what was really going on, all I had to do was ask that old blind street preacher, Mary Sweetwater. He said the whole thing had something to do with some kind of 'Great Event, The Miracle.' He told me the preacher could explain it all."

"Think she can?"

"Chief, after all that's happened tonight, I don't know *what* to think. All I know is something strange took place in that house tonight, something more powerful than all our semiautomatics."

"Well, Top', speaking of strange things..."

"Yeah?"

"For the past twenty four hours the department hasn't received a single 911 call. Not one. No muggings. Stabbings. Car jackings. Domestic violence. Purse snatchings. You know, the usual stuff that keeps the switchboard lit up on Christmas Eve. But like I said, *not one call*. Top', I'm a twenty-year veteran, and I've never seen a Christmas Eve like this one."

"Well," Topper sighed, "Who knows, Chief, maybe one day what happened tonight won't be a mystery any more; it'll be made plain. And we'll all understand."

"Yeah, Top'...maybe so...maybe so."

✳ *Chapter Twenty-Three*

Doctor Gilford Malliki O'Riley, majority stock holder, "Master Meteorologist" and founder of Riley's Weather Enterprises, arose early Christmas morning. His weather service, the most accurate and respected in the industry, was subscribed to by ninety percent of U.S. Media. The famed forecaster looked out his window. His prediction for the day called for gale-force winds, near-freezing temperatures, followed by morning blizzards -- snow accumulation, "a minimum of six inches."

Beyond the meteorologist's window spanned a spring-like sky. Aqua-blue. Cloudless. Sun-drenched. Where was the predicted Siberian weather?

Promenaders on Connecticut Avenue and at The Mall near the Reflecting Pool wore summer attire. Hundreds sat on the grass near the Washington Monument enjoying picnics, while on the Southwest waterfront, middle-aged anglers in shirt sleeves cast fishing lines.

Doctor O'Riley was stunned. Hurriedly, he raised the window and stuck out his hand. He estimated the temperature to be about eighty degrees. *Eighty?* The warmth was a repudiation of his state-of-the-art forecasting models. For the first time in his illustrious career, his forecast was wrong, not only wrong, but off by a colossal fifty or so degrees, at least.

"What's going on?" he puzzled. Later he'd discover it was the most extraordinary Christmas Day in Washington weather history, for by noon, a new temperature record was set -- eighty-seven degrees, in the shade. It was as if, Dr. O'Riley pondered, all classical weather indices had been flipped upside down and the science of meteorology didn't make sense anymore -- at least as it applied to Washington, DC on that unique Christmas Day.

Blocks away, Mrs. Alice Foster tapped on the door of Blind Reverend Mary's room.

"Mary, you up?" No answer. "Gorgeous day out! Thought it'd be nice if we went for a walk, enjoy a little of this fine spring-like weather. Come on, rise and shine, girl."

From the other side of the door, silence.

"Mary, come on, get up now." The preacher and Alice were close friends, had been for years. They often took walks together.

"Mary!"

More silence.

"Reverend, are you *alright?*." Anxiety now

strained Alice's voice. "Reverend! Reverend!"

Still, no answer.

Pivoting, the middle-aged woman hurried to the head resident's office. Soon, she and Mr. Woods stood in front of Mary's room.

He pounded the door.

"Hear anything?" Alice asked, watching as Mr. Woods leaned forward.

"Not a sound. Not like Mary at all, is it?"

"Sure isn't."

"Usually by now she's up, playing her radio, singing hymns. Mary! you in there? Say something!" She didn't.

Mr. Woods plucked a key from a large brass ring attached to his belt and unlocked the door. He and Mrs. Foster rushed in, abruptly slowed, then stopped. Both gazed, unable to believe what they saw. Before them, slumped in her easy chair, Blind Mary sat. Head angled. Eyes closed. Hands in her lap. Across their upturned palms lay a Bible.

"Oh my God!" Alice shrieked. "No-o-o! *Not* Mary!" The hysterical woman rushed to her friend's side. Hurriedly she pressed an ear to Mary's lips, listened, then frowned. She checked the preacher's pulse and heartbeat. Finding none, she again frowned. "Mary," she heaved, "she's dead!"

"No, no, not...dead?" Mr. Woods said.

"Afraid so."

"That's impossible! Mary's always been in such excellent health, up and about everyday, active, a dynamo. I just can't believe she's dead."

"You're not the only one. Why, just last week

after she went for her physical, she told me how pleased the doctor was. He said she had the body of a woman half her age, predicted she'd live to be at *least* a hundred."

"Well," Mr. Woods sighed, "guess that won't be." He shook his head. "Alice, there's at least one consolation: Mary died the way she'd have liked, *Good Book* in her hands."

"That's for sure." Alice eyed the corpse. "Whole thing's so mystifying. I mean, that someone in the best of health like Mary, should all of a sudden and for no apparent reason, just keel over! Makes no sense. Wait. You don't suppose some wicked agent of Satan poisoned her, do you? That happened last month to a woman over on McCormack Road, near Catholic University. Anyway, this whole thing looks mighty suspicious to me."

"Me too."

"Just thought, I got a friend who works in the coroner's office," Alice said. "Think I'll see if he can arrange to have an autopsy done."

"Sure can't do no harm."

Two hours later, Alice was on the telephone dialing Tim Thomas, a worker in the DC Coroner's Office. After telling him what had happened, she asked for his help.

"No problem. My guess is if the body's brought in today, doc' should have a full report by tomorrow noon at the latest. I'll stop by on my way home and give you the results."

"Would you, Tim'?"

"Sure, no problem."

At around six the following evening, Tim tapped on Alice's door.

She opened it and said, "Care to come in?"

"Thanks, but not this time. My wife and I plan to go out for dinner."

"Oh. So, tell me, what'd the coroner say?"

"Alice, doc' is just as mystified as you about why that woman died. Tests showed all her organs were functioning properly. No traces of poison, evidence of trauma, not a thing. Heart, liver, kidney, spleen...in excellent shape. As far as doc' could determine, your friend should be alive this very moment, maybe standing here chatting with us."

Alice shook her head. "Tim, what can I say? I ask, how do you explain something like this? I mean, my best friend drops dead on Christmas day, a time of birth and revival...and the coroner, with all his books and fancy machines, doesn't have the *faintest* idea why -- clueless."

"Alice, let's face it, what we humans know is, at best, limited, and there are things that happen even scientists can't explain."

"That's for sure. Tim, I just thought of something."

"What?"

"Sorta strange, but when I found Mary's body, she had a kind of odd expression. Never saw anything like it. She looked happy, Tim, joyfully so. Happier than I'd ever seen her when she lived and, as you know, in spite of her blindness, she was always a happy person. Anyway, she looked like some weary worker whose shift is over and is told to end her labors and return home."

"Um-m-m."

"Gives a body something to think about, doesn't it?"

"Yeah, it does. Well, Alice, guess I'd better be getting home. Sure hope what little information I brought you was helpful."

"It was, Tim, more than you know, because now I believe I understand why, though in perfect health, Mary died...and on Christmas Day."

"You say you understand, Alice? I certainly wish you'll explain it to me and the coroner."

"Tim, I'm not sure either of you'd believe me if I did. Anyway, thanks for all your help, and ah, merry Christmas."

"Merry Christmas, Alice."

Timmy left. Outside, he inhaled deeply, filling his lungs with unprecedentedly balmy Christmas air. Where, he chuckled, was the blizzard the noted meteorologist Dr. O'Riley promised? Where the freezing winds? What about the "minimum" six inches of snow? With his coat slung over is arm, he smiled as he savored the summer-like temperature. He was sure Blind Mary would have loved it also. But of course, she couldn't: she was dead, And his boss, a world-renowned pathologist, could explain her death about as successfully as Dr. O'Riley could tell why Washington, DC was enjoying June-like temperature on Christmas Day.

✳ *Chapter Twenty-Four*

Several days had passed since the 'Great Event," or, as increasing numbers called it, "The Miracle Birth."

The time was seven fifty-nine P.M. The meeting was scheduled to begin at eight, precisely. Fifty, or so, distinguished religious leaders had assembled. On the pulpit, a lone figure sat, Reverend Doctor Luther P. Pentagrass, president of the prestigious Washington-Baltimore Ministerial Alliance.

From his inside jacket pocket, the noted theologian removed a silk handkerchief and, dabbing his brow with it, coughed politely. He glanced at his Rolex. Always punctual, he rose, plucked an alien thread from his lapel, and, thumbs hooked in vest pockets, strode to the podium. Once there, he cleared his throat, scanned the audience and waited for the murmuring to subside. Finally, he spoke.

"Fellow ministers, allow me to thank you for assembling on such short notice. Be advised, I'm quite mindful of your pressing schedules. Those who know me realize I would not have requested your presence if the issue before this body was not of the greatest urgency."

Two days following the birth of Louella's baby, members of the richly-endowed Washington-Baltimore Ministerial Alliance, WBMA, were notified by its chairman, Dr. Pentagrass, of an important "specially-called meeting."

The meeting site was The Sixteenth Street Washington National Memorial Cathedral. Spanning two city blocks, the Gothic edifice, largest of its kind in North America, was just south of the Maryland line, in the affluent "Gold Coast" neighborhood.

"Rest assured," the chairman continued, "the meeting will be brief."

"Sure hope so," Bishop Lazarus Johnson grinned from the front row. "Our business is *saving* the suffering, not *suffering* the saved." Everyone chuckled.

"Lazarus," the chairman smiled, "I'm fully aware you'd raise the dead, as the Savior did your namesake, and raise something hotter, too, if we're not out of here speedily." Sprinkles of laughter.

"But seriously, fellow members, as stated, I intend to keep these proceedings brief, shouldn't last more than ten minutes at the most."

"Like God, we love brevity," someone inserted.

"Good. So, gentlemen," Doctor Pentagrass said, dabbing his brow with a handkerchief, "without further ado, I'll move swiftly to the point. We are all aware of what took place Christmas Eve in the house at Fourteenth and U."

"Indeed!" a voice detonated. "Indeed!"

"God's...blessing!"

"Amen. A *miraculous gift* to us all."

"It is in connection with that event," the chairman said, "that I requested your presence. Fellow members, with your indulgence I would like to submit a proposal. Needless to say, it is the obligation of The Alliance to commemorate the glorious occurrence that took place in that house. To memorialize the site, I recommend that this body set aside sufficient funds, raise additional if necessary, though it shouldn't be, to, one, purchase, then demolish the structure where the child was born.

"As you and I know, the house and the illegal purposes for which it was used, is an effrontery to the glory of Christmas and the goodness for which it stands. And two, in place of this residence of shame, I propose we erect a church, one the nation can take pride in. One with statuary, stained glass windows, and pews crafted from the finest oak."

"Splendid idea!" Bishop Richfield exploded, popping to his feet. "*Splendid!*"

"I endorse it wholeheartedly!" someone added.

"Indeed, an appropriate tribute to Christmas virtues."

Affirmations exploded, echoing like pistol fire. Acceptance of the proposal seemed certain. However, amid the blizzard of exclamations, a lone member of the assemblage sat near the rear. He remained silent, calm, seemingly unaffected by the exuberance swirling around him. Few noticed him, for he was quite ordinary, to the point of being banal.

Unlike that of others present, his clothing was "common," trite. His jacket, trousers, shirt, all unremarkable. He sported no gold rings, costly timepieces, cufflinks, or jewelry of any kind. Though he wore a tie, it, like his jacket and trousers, was frayed, most of its useful life now history.

"Ah, Mr. Chairman!"

"Does the gentleman in the rear wish recognition?"

"I do." The man stood. Whispers rippled. Heads turned.

"You'll have to forgive me, sir," Doctor Pentagrass said, "though I think I know all members of the Alliance, I'm afraid I don't recognize you."

"Few do, and those who do often deny the fact."

"It's just that I cannot place the face. Tell me, sir, are you a member of The Alliance?"

"No, not of yours, but I hold membership in a greater one, whose emissaries spoke of me in earlier times. Their names, all one dozen, I'm sure you gentlemen are familiar with."

"In other words, you *are* a minister?"

"So I have been called."

"I see. Ah, of what denomination, sir?"

"All."

"All?" the chairman puzzled.

"...And none."

Furrowing his brow, Dr. Pentagrass shrugged. "I understand, I...I..think."

"If only you did."

"Pardon. What was that?"

"Ah, nothing, Mr. Chairman. A mere aside to myself."

"Oh. Ah, Reverend, forgive me. I'm afraid I didn't get the name."

"Wasn't given."

"So, would you be so kind as to share your name with this body?"

"My name? It is a name often heralded under bloodstained banners of false righteousness."

"Kindly, sir, your name."

"My name?"

"Yes."

"It is a name cited at Christmas by present-givers, claiming they offer love, but know not what it is, believing it is something bought and gift-wrapped."

"Sir, would you *kindly* give us your name."

"Mr. Chairman."

"Yes."

"The truth is, my name is not important, but what it *stands for* is."

"Look, ah, if you wish to remain anonymous, that, of course, is your prerogative. At any rate, reverend, whether you are a member of this alliance or not, or want to or don't want to give your name, we're none the less delighted to share your fellowship."

"And I, yours, but too often I've been excluded."

"At any rate, reverend, the floor is yours."

"Thank you. First, Mr. Chairman, let me applaud your proposal to memorialize the site of the child's birth. Like you and others present, I share the conviction that the world must *never* forget the event, where it took place, or when, on Christmas Eve, and among whom, the lowly and lost. However, my proposal for memorializing the site is unlike yours."

"Unlike, you say?"

"Yes, Mr. Chairman."

"Would you kindly explain in what way?"

"I'd be delighted to. Sir, I recommend that under no circumstances, I repeat, *no circumstances*, should you demolish the house at Fourteenth and U. On the contrary, it is your obligation to see that the structure be preserved, *exactly* as it stood that most remarkable Christmas Eve. Not a single rafter or nail should be removed, not one room disturbed -- especially that in which the child was born. Even graffiti, outside and inside, should *remain* -- every syllable.

"And why? So that future generations can view the authentic site where Yuletide's hope returned, see for itself that Christmas goodness can exist *any* place -- the worst included -- among *any* people, even among, and especially, the lost, scorned and forgotten. Man's progeny deserves visual proof that the birth occurred, not among the *rich* and *mighty*, but the *wretched*, those who grapple daily with their demons. In a word, gentlemen, I propose the now-consecrated house at Fourteenth and U stand as a reminder that Christmas hope and love are not quenched, but live on, as they must...always."

Opposition to the strange man's proposal was immediate and vociferous.

"Shame! Outrageous!"

"Worse, blasphemous!"

"The man's a heretic."

"No, a loony!"

"Both," Bishop Richfield corrected. "Why, the very idea that a house of sin become a symbol of Yuletide's glories? *Unthinkable!*"

"Gentlemen...gentlemen!" Doctor Pentagrass pleaded, pounding his gavel. "Order, order! Please, let us have order. We waste precious time. Again, I direct your attention to my original proposal, now with an addendum: namely, that we commission the demolition of the house to begin as soon as possible, to be exact, this coming month."

The chairman paused and looked at the stranger. "Ah, Reverend, do you have further comments before I put my proposal in motion form and then to vote?"

"Yes, if you'd be so kind. I would like to go on record as saying that if you tear down the house at Fourteenth and U, you miss the point of what took place there and its significance to Christmas." The speaker paused. "Scholars of scripture as all you gentlemen are, I don't have to lecture you about why the birth occurred on Christmas Eve, in a, so-called, 'undesirable house in a bad neighborhood,' among those without means or hope." Again he paused. "Or...do I?" He waited for a response. None came.

"Is that all you wish to say?" the chairman asked.

"With your indulgence, permit me a final word."

"Do be brief."

"I shall. Gentlemen, a quotation from *First Kings* comes to mind. You I'm sure are familiar with it. It reads, in part, '*I have hallowed this house which thou has built...And mine heart shall be there...perpetually.*' The child's gift of Christmas hope and love, gentlemen, resides in that house, and that house alone, as the structure stands today, and as it stood that historical Christmas Eve. Not in some showy replacement, as you would have it. But only in the authentic, so-called, 'house of shame,' in that now majestic and sacred tenement where a welfare mother birthed a new beginning for Christmas, and, I add, fresh hope for all mankind.

"Spare the house, gentlemen, I beseech you. By saving it, you save the hope of Christmases to come, as well as hope for your children and theirs. For without the authentic house as a reminder, tomorrow's generations will surely return Yuletide to what it was: a hollow ritual of cold commerce."

The silence that followed exploded like a bomb.

"Are you...you through, sir?"

"I am, Mr. Chairman, except to say, gentlemen...the decision now rests in your hands. May wisdom guide you to make the proper choice."

With deliberate steps, the man moved down the aisle towards the exit. All eyes followed. Reaching the door, he paused, looked back, then, just as mysteriously as he had entered, he disappeared into the night.

No one ever saw the man again. Nor had he been seen prior to his appearance that night. To this day his identity remains a topic of speculation. He was ascribed a host of identities Some said he was the incarnation of the Christmas Spirit -- "odder things have happened," these argued. Others claimed he was Yuletide's patron saint, Saint Nicholas, risen from his grave, because he was angered that Christmas had been converted into a money machine. Some few were convinced the stranger was an escapee from a mental institution, no doubt a psychotic, which explained why he spoke in riddles.

A few, called the "lunatic fringe," even went so far as to say the stranger was God. Not many believed that, arguing that certainly The Supreme Being had better things to do with his valuable time than personally intervene in the razing of a rundown house in a "bad neighborhood."

Opponents countered that though the man admittedly seemed odd and spoke in strange ways and was unfashionably dressed, unlike distinguished members of The Alliance, much of what he said made sense. And, it turned out, some of his words proved to be prophetic, for, as he recommended, the house at Fourteenth and U, over The Alliance's objections, remained standing -- and still does today -- *exactly* as it did that Christmas Eve when it was transformed into a revered site.

✳ *Chapter Twenty-Five*

Following the birth of the child, those closest to the event went their separate ways. Their lives followed a maze of twists and turns, some anticipated, others impossible to foresee.

Snake no longer pursued a life of crime. To the astonishment of fellow hoods, and the regrets of local fences, he started his own business. To the astonishment of the DC Police Department, it was a legitimate one. He began peddling hamburgers from a little cart on the corner of Seventh and T.

"I promised my momma, I mean, my *real* momma, Blind Mary, I'd right some of the wrongs I've done. And the Good Lord knows I've done my share. Reverend Mary made me believe I had some worth, that I could change, make something of my life, be somebody. And in remembrance of that precious woman, come hell or high water, I *will*."

Within two years, the former hustler and con-man-turned-hamburger vendor was the owner of two thriving restaurants. Months later he launched five additional eateries, three in the District and two in affluent Montgomery County.

In record time Snake parlayed a little pushcart and a novel idea for a sandwich into a multimillion dollar enterprise trading on The New York Stock Exchange. Business couldn't have been better. A Legg Mason sector manager predicted that within two years Snake's company, SNA Enterprises, would rival McDonald's in net earnings. It did, but in fewer than six months.

Last year, the pastor of Saint Jude's Church on upper Wisconsin Avenue, Reverend Arthur DeLite, reported an incident that baffled him. Saint Jude's was the church from which Snake and Super stole needy children's Christmas toys.

Reverend DeLite said a week before Christmas an eight-wheeler owned by a local moving company, DC Transfer, lumbered to a halt in front of his church. The driver and his crew unloaded a massive assortment of new toys, then stacked the playthings in the basement of the church. Estimated retail value? Over seventy thousand dollars, far more than the worth of the toys stolen by Snake and Super. The pastor asked the driver who the benefactor was, but received no answer -- at least none he could make sense of.

"Mister, all I do is follow orders, and my orders was to drop this load off, then read a note to-ya."

"A note?"

"Yes, sir. Be right back."

The delivery man stepped to his rig and returned with a clipboard. On it was clamped a typed note. "*'Dear Reverend DeLite,'*" the driver read, " *'This Christmas, please have Santa deliver these toys to children he would otherwise forget, as he once forgot me. I'm sorry I'm late in donating them, but the truth is, some learn the meaning of Christmas slower than others, and I'm one such person.*

"*'In addition, I'd like you to do me a special favor. Please get a message to one who years ago was on your Santa list. Jimmy Ragland is his name. I hope his name and address are still in your files. Tell Jimmy I'm sorry I denied him something dear to childhood -- the joy of a -Santa-visited Christmas morning. Also, tell him his college education will be paid for -- regardless of costs. To me, Reverend, money is no object, my peace of mind is.*

"*'You're probably wondering what my connection to Jimmy is. It would shame me to tell you, as it shames me to think of who I once was, and the things I once did. And for too long, I've carried that shame on my shoulders...and in my heart.*

"*'I recently established The Jimmy Ragland Foundation. Through it, your church will receive Christmas toys for needy children to the end of the next millennium.*

"*'I funded another endowment. Some of its monies will anonymously be given to your church to aid down and out widows. I named it The Widow Flossie Robinson Fund, in honor of an angel of a woman whose sad death bothers me even today. But hers is another story, one I can't find words to*

tell -- perhaps there are none. Respectfully.'"
"Ah, who wrote that?" the clergyman wanted
to know.
"Can't tell-ya."
"Won't you even give me a...hint?"
"Wish I could, reverend."
"I...see."
Unknown to Reverend DeLite, the driver was
sworn to secrecy. If he divulged the writer's identity,
a "certain influential businessman" threatened to
acquire controlling interest in DC Transfer, then
terminate its entire staff.
Many said Snake was the anonymous donor.
Hearing the rumor and seeing the possibility of a
good human interest story, a reporter for *The
Washington Post* asked the successful businessman if
in fact he were the benefactor.
"Me?" Snake shrugged, being interviewed in
the back seat of his chauffeured stretch limo. "*Me?*
Do a thing like that? Come on, lady, I'm a business
man. Besides, folks used to call me Snake.
Remember?"
With a nod, the entrepreneur signaled his
chauffeur, Charles, indicating it was time to head for
the business seminar the multimillionaire was
sponsoring. Charles flipped the ignition key and the
powerful V-8 roared to life. As the limousine, minus
the journalist, purred up Connecticut Avenue, Snake
complained to Charles that he had wasted "valuable
time" answering the reporter's "dumb" questions.
"Me? Give away that kind of money...to...to children
and old women? Ridiculous! I'm not Santa Claus!"

Later, as Charles opened the door for his employer, he noticed that Mr. Johnson's eyes watered.

"Are you alright, sir? You seem to be crying."

"I'm...I'm fine, Charles. Must be my... allergies acting up."

"Well, it's certainly allergy season alright."

"Yes, it is. By the way, have a merry Christmas, Charles," the mogul said, handing his chauffeur a bulging envelope.

"Thank you, sir. As always, you're *more* than generous."

"My pleasure."

"You are indeed a good man. I have seen the *many* kind things you've done for the less fortunate, especially at Christmas, yet you refuse to take credit for doing them."

"Charles."

"Yes, sir."

"If only you could know the man I *used* to be. I'm sure you wouldn't believe anyone could be such a person. Sometimes I don't believe it myself. Anyway, I should be leaving in about two hours."

"I'll be waiting, sir. And I hope your allergies get better."

"Allergies? I don't have aller... Oh, yes, that, of course, my allergies. How could I forget?"

"Um, is odd you'd forget. Probably just a slip of the mind."

"Yes, Charles...just a slip of the mind."

Chicago Red, who operated the shooting gallery

where Louella's baby was born, soon returned to his parents' small, struggling farm. Few knew it, but Red wasn't really from Chicago, though he always boasted he was. Being from The Windy City lent, he felt, a certain sophistication and toughness to his persona. Because he wanted to be perceived as street wise and a member of the "criminal crowd," he led everyone to believe he'd "blown in" from "Chi' Town"; sometimes forgetting, he said it was from The Big Apple. Neither, of course, was true.

Red also misrepresented his real name. He didn't like it -- Dale Otha Potts -- so he claimed his legal name was Tony Red, street names, Chicago, Chicago Red, or to friends, plain, Red. But whether Chicago, Chicago Red, Red, Tony Red, or, legally, Dale Otha Potts, he was actually from Suqualena, a sleepy hamlet a few miles outside of Meridian, Mississippi. It was here he returned, not to the Windy City.

Eighty, nearly blind and totally deaf, John Henry Potts, Red's father, was no longer able to work the family farm, a small parcel of once-profitable land. The property had been in the family for generations and was the old man's prized possession.

Red took over its operation. Absent from the physical demands of farm work for years, he found the transition painful. Until his body adjusted, his back ached and hands smarted from painful calluses.

In time, however, the discomfort disappeared and the one-time shooting gallery operator settled into his new life as a farmer.

Months later, a former junkie and one of the few who knew where Red's true home was, "Tiddy Mouse" (Silas Jones) journeyed to Suqualena to visit his "ole buddy." Tiddy reported the man he found there was not the same one he'd known during his daily visits to the infamous house at Fourteenth and U. Red, he told friends, was a "new person,": he seemed more at ease, no longer warring with the world or himself.

Tiddy said Red asked about his "old customers" and hoped they and heaven would forgive him for the role he played in their lives, profiting from their misery. He wished them God's speed and prayed they would "sign a truce" with themselves, as he had. His reconciliation came like a flash, Red said, when he stepped into the room at Fourteenth and U that Christmas Eve and saw Louella cuddling, what he called, "the Miracle Child." At that instant, he told Tiddy, something inside him shifted like a heavy weight. Seeing mother and baby, he was somehow given, what he called, "the greatest Christmas present a man can receive -- peace with himself."

Following the birth, Sweet Lucy, Louella's midwife, struggled to salvage what little remained of her life. She enrolled in a drug rehabilitation program, something she had done before -- nine times, to be exact. But with each try her demons repossessed her, dragging the former nurse deeper into drug-induced nightmares.

This latest attempt, however, would be different,

Sweet assured. And she was right. Until her death, she remained "clean." She worked as a janitress at the DC Consolidated Office Complex on K Street. Upon learning she was once a crack head with a police record, no hospital in the region would hire her as a nurse, what she was trained to be.

Sweet lived a modest life. Married a few years ago, she confided to her husband, Tony Goodman, that she had but one dream: to become, "like Louella, a loving, caring mother." Months later, Doctor Larry Adams gave Sweet and her husband the "good news, bad news." Good news -- Sweet carried a child. Bad news -- she was HIV positive.

Sweet decided to have her baby anyway. The good news was that her baby was born healthy, testing negative for HIV. In tribute to the man who, Sweet said, saw her as a human being when the world didn't see her at all, she named her baby "Willie." A dynamo of health, the infant sparkled energy.

But Sweet, now in the final stages of AIDS, had little energy left. She treasured each week as if it were her last, as well it might have been. She was told she had two years to live.

Dr. Adams was amazed at how calmly she took the news. "Did you understand what I just said?"

"Every syllable."

"Oh. I wasn't sure I'd made myself clear."

"Look, Doc', I don't have to tell you drugs were my downfall. But strangely," she mused, hinting a smile, "it was because of drugs I happened to be in the *wrong* place, but at the *right* time one

Christmas Eve. And while destroying my own life, I helped bring a new one into the world, one with hope and promise, things I had little of. And, Doc', that I helped bring that *special* baby into the world gives me all the strength I'll need to face these final two years."

"Two or...less, Sweet. Probably...less."

"More...less," she shrugged, "matters not. Either way, thanks to my role in that baby's birth, I'm ready."

Sweet hoped the end would come peacefully. She told Dr. Adams she'd instructed her husband that at her funeral there were to be "no sad songs," only "happy ones that celebrate life."

When she died -- peacefully, as she had hoped -- Doctor Adams, who had been a family friend for years, attended her funeral.

He reported that as requested by the dead woman, there were no sad songs in the service, only uplifting melodies of hope.

✳ *Chapter Twenty-Six*

Following blizzards of feature stories in the local press about the "Miracle Birth" -- as well as national coverage by *The New York Times, The Wall Street Journal, National Inquirer*, etc. -- nearly everyone in America knew what happened to Louella's baby. But no one could definitively explain why it happened or exactly how -- not even the F.B.I.

Two weeks after Louella had her child, his corpse, wrapped in a World War 11 duffel bag, was found in The District in a dumpster behind the Eastern Ridge Apartment Complex, just off Nebraska Avenue. A male jogger reported seeing "a foreign-looking woman" speeding from the scene in a rusty, early model Chevrolet sedan, possibly a Nova.

At around noon the previous day someone kidnapped the baby and, from all available evidence, the child was soon thereafter murdered. Judging from abrasions on his neck, the cause of death was strangulation.

There followed a smorgasbord of theories claiming to explain events leading to, during, and following the baby's death. The most credible scenario, according to F.B.I. Special Agent Kenneth Rogers, focused on one Maria Del Rosa -- alias Martha Hodges, Gloria Sween, plus a slew of other fake names. Maria was a member of an itinerant band of career-criminal Gypsies. At the time of the child's birth, the group was "working" the DC metropolitan area: Montgomery, Howard and Prince George's counties.

The lawbreakers specialized in staged auto accidents, bogus home repairs, burglaries, fortune telling, and exorcism scams. Plus, anything else that happened their way, as long as it was profitable, required little or no work -- and was illegal.

Maria read about the "miracle birth" and schemed to kidnap the child. She planned to demand a huge ransom, six million dollars, not from the parents who, the news article said, were penniless, but from The Greater Washington Ministerial Alliance or, that failing, one of the affluent churches on upper Sixteenth Street. Another option was to appeal directly to the Pope or Reverend Billy Graham...or both.

Having kidnapped the baby, Maria envisioned herself wallowing in money. However, when she learned that the entire DC Detective Unit was assigned the case -- working around the clock, some without pay -- and that within hours the F.B.I. would join the search, it is believed she panicked. Hoping, authorities speculated, to "get rid of the evidence," she murdered the baby and tossed his body into a dumpster, then fled south.

Two days later, just outside Savannah, Georgia, in a sleazy motel, The Rebel Belle, a chamber maid found Maria's body in one of the inn's dingiest rooms. The female felon ended her life by angling the muzzle of a sawed-off shotgun into her mouth, then squeezing the trigger. A suicide note lay in her lap, partly covering the crucifix tattooed on the back of her right hand. *"All Mighty Father,"* the note read, *"forgive me, for in my madness for money, I murdered the innocent Christmas Child."*

Is this account accurate? The F.B.I. said, except for minor details, it is essentially correct. This much, however, is known with certainty: on the day of the abduction, two women appeared at Louella's door. (The Good Samaritan Missionary provided her and Willie lodging in an apartment in Southeast Washington.) The older of the two females fitted the description of Maria Del Rosa exactly, including the crucifix tattooed on the back of her right hand, and wording running the length of her left forearm, front and back, which read, "Suffer little children to come unto me, for such is the kingdom of God." It was the tattooed woman who asked for a glass of water. Louella stepped to the kitchen to fetch it. When she returned, the visitors were gone -- so was her baby.

Soon after the discovery of the child's body, police transported it to the coroner's office. The chief examiner was Dr. Wang Fou, a nationally acclaimed pathologist. Facing a backlog, he placed the remains in a storage drawer. His intention was to examine the body the first thing the following day. Early the next morning when he opened the drawer, he startled: the corpse was not there. He saw only the duffel bag and an impression of the child's body seemingly singed into its fabric.

Staring at the empty container, the pathologist was speechless.

Dr. Fou possessed the only key card to the morgue, one impossible to duplicate. He secured it on his person at *all* times. What's more, police reported there was no evidence of forced entry. No jimmy marks on the door or the lock. Hinges were in place, unmarred, windows secured by quarter inch steel bars. So how did the body vanish? And where had it gone?

The following day, the area in the drawer where the baby had lain, for some unexplained reason, was body-temperature warm. And it remains so even unto this day.

Henry "Brain" Nelson, a veteran private sleuth famed for solving cases DC detectives couldn't, was commissioned to investigate. Immediately he suspected Doctor Fou knew more about the missing corpse than he was telling. Brain theorized the coroner sold the remains to one of the leading medical research universities, Johns Hopkins or Harvard.

It was known in the medical community, the detective learned, that when Louella had her ultrasound, her fetus produced no image. Obstetricians and researchers worldwide were eager to study the "invisible baby." Some, according to inside sources, were prepared to acquire the cadaver by "any means necessary, no questions asked, no price too high."

Investigator Nelson asked Doctor Fou if he'd agree to take a polygraph test. Claiming he had nothing to hide, the pathologist willingly consented. The exam confirmed what the suspect contended all along -- he didn't have any idea what happened to the corpse. "It's as if," he puzzled, "the child's body no longer interacted with light, rendering it, as it would anything, invisible, as least, to...*human* eyes."

Scientists pondered how a corpse could vanish from a locked drawer, in a locked room, both secured by barred windows. In addition, cameras monitored the building's interior. Outside, two security guards patrolled. A review of the surveillance tapes showed nothing suspicious. The guards, both polygraphed, said they too saw nothing unusual.

One guard, however, said he "thought" he noticed a glow ascend from the morgue's roof at around four on the morning of the baby's disappearance. The polygraph operator questioning the guard was skeptical, suspecting the man, no doubt drowsy at the hour mentioned, "imagined" the incident. The examiner asked no further questions about the matter. His assistant believed he should have and convinced his boss to do so. Unfortunately, the guard who reported seeing the rising glow suffered a brain concussion the following day in a three car pileup on the Baltimore

Washington Parkway and died within hours, taking details of the mysterious light to his grave.

Meanwhile, the morgue drawer, heated by a mysterious radiation, remained warm, and the experts...baffled, and the whereabouts of Louella's baby...unexplained. The matter remains as puzzling today as it was when the corpse vanished...never to be seen again.

Or, as Dr. Fou suggested, never to be seen again by... "*human* eyes."

✴ *Chapter Twenty-Seven*

"Lou'."

"Yeah, Willie."

"Are you 'wake?"

"Sorta. What 'bout you?"

"Same here, Lou'...sorta."

"I just can't seem to doze off."

"Me neither. Can't explain it, but I feel kinda, you know, fretful and uneasy-like. I been just laying here...*thinking*, Lou."

"'Bout what, Willie?"

"About our son, and Blind Mary's prophesy of how he'd change Christmas...and people's hearts. I was thinking that now that he's dead, I suppose her predictions 'bout him can't come true after all."

"That ain't *necessary* so."

"Ain't? Why-ya say that, Lou'?"

"Kinda hard to explain. But here lately I've been having this strange feeling that, though he's dead, our child will do 'actly what the blind preacher said he would. It's a *strong* feeling, Willie, strongest I've *ever* known. Usually it come with a voice that sound like the howling of winter winds."

"This voice you speak of, explain it to me."

"Ain't sure I can, Willie. But like I said, it's there alright, and it tell me..."

"Yeah? Tell-ya what?"

"It tell me that our child's *death* won't matter none, Willie."

"Won't?"

"No."

"I...I don't understand."

"I mean, it won't matter as far as Blind Mary's prophesy go. What I'm saying is, though our baby's dead, things will turn out just like Mary told it."

"Think they will?"

"Sure."

"I mean *really*?"

"Couldn't be more certain."

"But, how you explain how a dead baby that nobody can't find is going to--"

"I can't...not in no *science* way. But, Willie, I ain't sure explaining it in a science way or any other way would make no difference."

"Why?"

"There be lotta things I can't explain in a science way, me or nobody else."

"True."

"Stuff like, you know, dreams, a mother's love and the darkness that clouds the hearts of some. Them college fellas, bet they can't explain stuff like that neither, but 'cause they can't, don't mean these things ain't real."

"Good point."

"So like I told-ya, Willie, the voice said because

of our son and folks' memory of him, there'll be goodness and joy in Christmas once again."

"That would be nice, Lou'. Might help to make up for the loss...the terrible pain of it all." Willie's long sigh was wobbly with emotion.

"Yes, good *has* to come outta' losing him."

"I sure hope-ya right."

"And there're other things the voice said, things that'll help me heal the hurt of losing my baby. Cause the pain that aches in my heart is worser than any thing I ever felt. My arms long to hold him. Sometimes I think the tears'll never stop."

"Tell me what else the voice said," Willie prompted as he touched her hand.

"It told me that every Christmas people will speak of our son and the gift he gave. What's more, the voice said that that comet folks saw will light up the sky every Christmas Eve just like it did when our child was born."

"All this sure is 'culiar, ain't it, Lou'?"

"It is that... And something else."

"Yeah?"

"The voice said that the crack house at Fourteenth and U will one day be honored like it's some kinda...*sacred place*, and when folks enter it they'll bow their heads and speak in whispers. And at Christmas, choirs from all over will gather before it and join in singing carols. There'll be *important* people who'll visit the house, even the *President* of The United States. And folks will line up for blocks to see the room where our baby was born."

"All-a this don't...don't seem *possible!*"

"The voice said more folks will visit the birth room of our child than will go to that big gattery down there on Constitution Avenue. Ah, what's its name?"

"The National Gattery of Art, I think."

"That sound 'bout right. Anyway, the voice said God-fearing folks from everywhere will honor that Fourteenth and U neighborhood."

"*That* neighborhood? You gotta be kidding, ain't-cha?"

"No, I ain't kidding, and I understand that what I'm saying ain't easy to believe, Willie."

"Like believing north is south or east is west."

"And there's something else. The voice said that you and me, Willie, we gonna be celebrated, too."

"Us? Celebrated?"

"Yes, celebrated."

"For what?"

"Don't ask me. Only guess I can make is, 'cause we was the child's parents."

"And we'll be celebrated for *that*?"

"What else could it be? For God knows, we just poor, common folks. We ain't done nothing special. Leastwise, I ain't."

"Same here."

"Anyway, them's the things the voice told me."

"Well, all I can say is they're hard to believe, no, near impossible. I mean, a *crack* house visited at Christmas by the President, choirs caroling in front of it, folks lining up to see the room where our baby was born; you and me, nobodies, celebrated, and a...murdered baby changing Christmas...and the hearts of folks. It's enough to *bust the brain.*"

"I know, Willie,...I know."

For several minutes they, holding hands, lay basking in silence, each contemplating the things discussed, things "too impossible" to come true.

Neither, of course, could look into the future. Had they been able to, they would have known that the "impossible" things would, in time, *all* come true. And that the old blind preacher was right: because of Louella's "special" baby and the once-notorious-soon-to-be-revered tenement at Fourteenth and U, Christmas and the lives of countless numbers would never be the same...*never.*

"Ah, you...you think you gon' be able to go to sleep now?"

"Yeah, probably."

"'Night, Willie."

"'Night, Lou'."

ISBN 141201384-4